BELIZE BLISS

C.L. COLLIER

Cover Design by Amy Queau, Q Designs

Editing by Jenny Sims, Editing 4 Indies

 Created with Vellum

I dedicate this book to Dee Snider of Twisted Sister.

Yes, you read that right.

We hope you enjoyed the Maya Beach Hotel as much as we did. You seemed to be enjoying The Bistro when we saw you dining there.

Rock on.

1

MONIQUE

"Welcome to Belize," the customs agent says as he hands my passport back to me. I stuff it into my purse, then turn and head in the direction I need to go.

It's been a long two days of traveling, and while I'm excited to finally be in Belize, I still have another flight to catch before I make it to my destination. I can't wait to arrive at the Maya Beach Hotel for a week of sun, fun, and relaxation. My parents, sister, and her boyfriend are already there, as well as the family friends who are joining us. I'm the last one to arrive, so to say I'm eager to get there is an understatement.

After exchanging euros for Belize dollars, I walk through a corridor to the other section of the airport to wait for my flight. This airport is nothing like I've been to before. For one, it's small, especially for an international airport. Two, all of the chairs to sit on are wooden slat pieces of furniture that look like they belong on a patio or out on a beach. And three, reggae Christmas music plays over the speakers.

It's not quite Christmastime yet since Thanksgiving is only two days away. That's the whole reason my family decided to travel here for the week. Mom and Dad wanted to do something different this year since my sister and I are grown and live away from our hometown. They thought it would be fun to have a destination Thanksgiving where we could all meet and make a vacation out of it. Then their best friends, the Blakes—who they've been friends with since my parents moved to the US—thought it sounded like a great idea, so Mom and Dad invited them to join us... along with their two sons.

I haven't seen Kyle or Kevin Blake since high school, so it's been well over ten years. I'm curious to see what they both look like now and what their lives are like. Kevin and I are the same age. Kyle is two years older than me, and he was always kind of a dick. He's good looking, and he knows it. He was always arrogant and had an attitude. I'm curious to meet his fiancée, who's also coming along on this trip. This is sure to be an interesting vacation.

I walk toward the gate where my flight will leave from. Several other people are milling about and sitting in chairs, waiting for their flight. I survey the scene and notice a walk-up bar across the way selling frozen daiquiris and margaritas. It's afternoon here, although the jet lag is already messing with me. I left Paris yesterday at five thirty in the evening, had an almost ten-hour flight to Atlanta, but arrived there at nine thirty Atlanta time. Then I stayed at a nearby hotel for the night and tried to get a good night's sleep before my flight left this morning. Now, I'm an hour behind Atlanta's time as well. I could definitely use a drink to help myself relax before my next flight departs, which isn't for another half hour, so I walk toward the bar.

"Hello," the Belizean bartender says with her Creole accent. "What can I get for you?"

I smile, then look at the flavors of frozen daiquiris they have churning in the machines. "I'll have a strawberry coconut daiquiri, please."

She smiles, then goes about getting my drink.

My phone vibrates in my pocket, so I take it out to see who it is. It's a text message from Mom.

"Here you go," the bartender says, setting my drink on the counter. "That'll be twelve dollars."

I rummage through my purse for my wallet, then take out fifteen Belize dollars and hand them to her. "Keep the change," I say as I pick up my drink.

"Thank you," she says with a smile.

With my daiquiri in hand, I walk back toward the gate and find an empty chair to sit. I take a sip of my drink and am pleasantly surprised by the delicious taste. I take another sip, then turn my attention to my phone to read my mom's text message.

> We can't wait to see you! Your dad and I will pick you up from the airport. Text me before your flight takes off. Love you!

> Okay, I will. Love you, too!

As a steelhead drums version of "Jingle Bells" plays

overhead, I take another sip of my daiquiri, then type out a text to my friend and coworker Becca. It's evening time in Paris, and she'll probably be going to bed soon. I'm curious to know how business was the past couple of days at my store. I own a clothing boutique, Lavender Lace, which I opened a few years ago after moving to Paris. Although I was born in France and have dual citizenship, I didn't grow up there; however, I call it home now.

I grew up in Southern California. Both of my parents are originally from Paris, though, and they moved back for a short time before I was born. They got pregnant with me, and I was born there before they decided to settle in California. I was only a few months old, so I don't remember living there as a child, but we took several trips to visit throughout my childhood. After my mom's parents passed away, my parents inherited their house, which they used as a vacation home once or twice a year when they could make a trip to France. However, I saw it as an opportunity to make my dream of living in Paris and opening my own store a reality, and I convinced my parents to let me live in the house full time. While I do miss my family and friends in the States, I don't regret moving to Paris for one minute.

My parents still live in the same house I grew up in. My sister, Adeline, moved to Chicago for her job, where she met her boyfriend, Andre. I've met him a handful of times, and he seems perfect for Adeline. I look forward to spending more time with him and my sister over the next week.

Becca replies to my text, so I swipe my phone screen to read it.

Everything at the store is going great! The past couple of days we had some good sales. You're on vacation—you shouldn't be worrying about the shop! Have fun!

I chuckle because I knew Becca would say that. I'm a workaholic, and if it wasn't for her, I'd be buried in work. Sure, I could've found another person to fill her role if she hadn't walked into my shop that day, but I'm so grateful she did.

As I wait for my flight to start boarding, I scroll through social media on my phone and sip on my daiquiri. Adeline posted pictures of the hotel we're staying at, and it looks amazing. As I swipe through her photos, though, I also come across a few of her, Andre, and my parents on a small plane... a *really* small plane... and then I realize...

"Now boarding Tropic Air flight 3755 to Placencia," someone with a Creole accent says over the loudspeaker. I look up and see people lining up at the gate. This is my flight, but now I'm terrified after seeing Adeline's pictures.

I suck the rest of my drink down. I'll need the liquid courage to board this plane if it's as small as what was in Adeline's pictures. I knew I'd be flying on a smaller propeller plane from here to Placencia, but I expected it to be a little bigger.

Standing, I toss my empty cup into a nearby garbage can before joining the short line for flight 3755. There aren't a lot of people... because this plane won't hold that many.

The line starts walking out, and before I know it, I'm standing on the runway, looking at a single-propeller plane that looks like something used for air tours, not commercial flights. What have I gotten myself into?

As I follow the line of passengers toward the plane, my heart pounds in my chest. I can't believe *this* is the plane I have to ride on. I have enough anxiety flying on large jets. Nothing debilitating or anything—just your average anxiety I think most people get when flying—but this is different. If anything goes wrong on this small plane, we're all doomed. After all, having only one propeller on this thing means there's no backup if it fails.

The people in front of me start climbing the stairs to board. I wring my sweaty palms together, close my eyes, and say a quick, silent prayer that this flight makes it safely to Placencia. I'm not religious, but I always feel the need to pray before flying, which seems necessary in this case.

As I climb the steps and board the plane, I'm astonished once again at how small the cabin is. I can't even stand because the ceiling is so low. Hunched over, I make my way to a seat only two seats behind the cockpit... which has no partition from the rest of the seats in the cabin. The pilots are just there, all the flying equipment open to the passengers. What the hell? Is this legal? If someone wanted to hijack this thing, it wouldn't be difficult.

Well, maybe it would be a little difficult, considering you can't even stand straight inside. In fact, there's not a lot of room to move around at all. And I'm about to take off in this thing?

I buckle my seat belt, and the woman sitting next to me smiles kindly before turning her head to look out the window. I'm on the aisle seat, but I still have a clear view out the window... as well as the windshield just a couple of rows ahead of me.

The door is closed behind us, then one of the two pilots sitting up front starts the engine. The single propeller whirls to life. Holy shit, this is really about to happen? I'm putting my life in these two pilots' hands, hoping this toy plane arrives safely at the Placencia airport.

There's no safety presentation. Not that there could be... there's nowhere for a flight attendant to stand to give one. Actually, there's no flight attendant. It's just the two pilots and the—I quickly count how many of us are on board—twelve of us passengers filling up this plane.

We lurch forward and taxi to the runway. I close my eyes, take a deep breath, and say another silent prayer. I don't remember the last time I've prayed so frequently in such a short amount of time.

Suddenly, the plane races forward. We're already on the runway, ready to take off. I feel like I'm riding inside a roller skate. This is the smart car of planes, and I'm about to fly through the air for the next half hour in this thing!

The wheels lift off the ground, and we start to ascend. Holding my breath, I close my eyes and say another silent prayer. The engine is loud, but I hear other passengers around me talking. When one of them says, "What an incredible view," I have to open my eyes to look.

And I'm glad I do. Although my nerves are still a wreck, imagining this tiny plane crashing to the ground in flames, the view is spectacular. The Caribbean Sea is sparkling from the sun, and I'm surprised by how green

Belize actually is. I'm also surprised to see mountains in the distance. Obviously, I didn't study much about Belize before this trip. It truly is beautiful from however many feet high we are right now, and the scene surprisingly calms my nerves a bit.

Somehow, I manage to enjoy the flight, and before I know it, we're landing... onto the smallest airstrip at the smallest airport I've ever seen. Once we land and come to a stop at the other end of the runway, the pilot has to do a U-turn to get back to the airport, which literally consists of two small buildings—one for Tropic Air and the other for Maya Air, which is the other airline that flies between cities in Belize.

This is the craziest travel experience I've ever had.

The pilot parks the plane in front of the Tropic Air building, and an airline worker comes out to open the plane's exit door. "Welcome to Placencia," he says to all of us aboard, and then everyone starts to disembark.

As I make my way off the plane, I notice a couple of workers taking our luggage out from the underbelly of the plane and piling it all onto a large hand-pulled cart. I follow the other passengers to a waiting area outside the small Tropic Air building.

"Wait here for your luggage," an airline worker tells us.

It doesn't take long for them to finish unloading our bags, and one of the workers pulls the large cart over to where all of us wait. He checks our baggage claim tickets as we take our luggage. Once I have mine, I wheel it around to the front of the building to see if my parents are here yet. I have no idea what their rental car looks like, but considering how small this parking lot is, I'm sure they'll see me if I don't see them first.

"Monique!" I hear Mom's voice, then see her waving across the parking lot.

I head toward her, and my dad gets out of the silver Chevy SUV rental car. "Hi!" I say as my mom and I embrace. It's been months since we've seen each other, so it feels good to be together again.

"It's so good to see you!" Mom holds me tight, lightly rubbing my back.

When we finally release one another, I instantly turn to my dad and hug him as well. "Hello, ma fille chérie," he says, which is what he's always called Adeline and me. It means "my dear daughter" in French.

"Hi, Dad," I say, holding him a bit longer before we let go.

"How was your flight?" Mom asks.

I laugh. "Well, honestly, that last flight was a bit nerve-racking on that toy airplane!"

Mom and Dad laugh, then Dad replies, "We were surprised by how small it was, too."

"Wait until you see our hotel," Mom says as Dad takes my suitcase. "You're going to love it. It's right on the beach!"

As Dad puts my suitcase in the back of the SUV, Mom and I get in. She sits up front, and I sit right behind her.

"How far is the hotel from here?" I ask as Dad gets in the driver's seat.

"About fifteen minutes," Mom replies, and I'm grateful it's not too far.

As Dad drives along the two-lane road, I'm surprised

by what I see. There are lots of trees, a couple of nice hotels along the way, and many shacks where locals live. When we approach a small village, I'm shocked at the poverty I see. Kids play in the street barefoot. Shacks are built on stilts and look patched together with various metal and wooden materials. It's unlike anything I've ever seen before, and I'm not sure how to feel about it. My heart goes out to these people. I feel foolish having not researched this country more before arriving. I thought everything here would be a tropical paradise.

When Dad pulls up to the Maya Beach Hotel, I must admit it's not exactly what I expected either. There's not a parking lot, just parking spaces in front of the various buildings that make up the hotel, as well as several trees lining the property.

"It doesn't look like much here," Mom says as we get out of the car. "But wait until you see your room and how close to the beach it is. It's amazing."

"Okay," I say, trusting my mom.

Dad gets my suitcase, and I follow Mom to the first building we come to, which is the open-air check-in desk. I'm already impressed by how much nicer it looks here than from the street. I walk up to the counter, where a blond woman works.

"Hello," she says. "Welcome to the Maya Beach Hotel." She has an American accent, and I wonder where she's from.

"Hi. My name is Monique Blanchet, and I'm checking in."

"Ah, yes, Ms. Blanchet. I have you in the Kingfish suite," she says. "How many keys would you like?"

"Just one is fine," I reply.

Mom pats my back as if she's comforting me, and I inwardly cringe. My mom would *love* to see me in a relationship and settle down soon, like Adeline. After all, she's three years younger than me, so why haven't I—the eldest daughter—found a man yet?

Ugh. I'm happy being single, thank you very much.

"Here you go," the blond woman says, sliding an actual key on a keychain—not a key card—across the counter toward me. "I'll show you to your room."

"Oh, okay," I say, surprised she's going to walk me there.

The woman walks around and meets us outside. Dad wheels my suitcase for me, and we follow her around the building. Once we get to the other side, my jaw drops. The beach is *right there* with the Caribbean Sea just a few yards away, small waves lapping against the shore. With palm trees lining the beach and the water a beautiful clear blue color, I feel as if I've entered the tropical paradise I envisioned. Dad lifts my suitcase and carries it as we walk across the sand toward the rooms. The blond woman leads us to a single building, which looks like a small beach hut with a deck on the front of it, facing the sea. She walks up the steps of the deck, and we follow.

"Here we are," she says, opening the door, then standing aside to let me enter first.

Holy crap. I truly am in a tropical paradise! As I walk in the door, I see the king-sized bed straight away. To the left is a small table and chairs, and to the right is a chaise lounge, a tall armoire, and a TV hanging on the wall. I walk farther into the room and find a kitchenette complete with a fridge, microwave, coffee maker, sink, and stove. The bathroom is just off the kitchenette.

"This is so cute," Mom says.

"Yeah, it is," I reply, realizing I'll be able to lie in bed and look straight out the sliding glass door at the beach. This is heaven.

"Can I get you anything else?" the woman asks.

I shake my head. "No, I don't think so. This room is perfect."

She smiles, seemingly glad to know I'm pleased with the accommodations. "Please don't hesitate to ask if you need anything. All the information you need to know about the hotel is in the paperwork on the table," she says, pointing at the papers.

"Thank you," I say before she leaves through the sliding glass door again. Then I turn to my parents, both standing in front of the armoire. "Where's your room?" I ask, curious to know if their room is like mine or a little different.

"It's just on the other side of this hut next to you. Actually, I think Kevin might be staying in that hut," Mom says.

"Our building has four units," Dad says. "Ours is upstairs, and so is Dan and Kathy's room. Adeline and Andre's room is below ours, and Kyle and his fiancée's is below Dan and Kathy's."

Oh, so the four couples are in one building, and Kevin

and I—the singles—are in individual huts? I'm sure it's just a coincidence the way it worked out, but still. Funny.

"Sarah. Kyle's fiancée's name is Sarah," Mom adds before looking at her watch. "It's only two o'clock. I know you're tired, and I am, too. I think I'm going to take a nap before dinner."

"What are the plans for dinner?" I ask.

"Everyone's meeting at five thirty at the hotel's restaurant, The Bistro," Mom says. "So you can relax before it's time to meet."

"Adeline, Andre, and the Blakes are all out kayaking," Dad says.

"Oh, okay." I'm kind of bummed I can't see my sister yet, but that's okay. I *am* tired, so having time to relax before dinner sounds great.

Mom gives me another hug. "We'll see you a little later, honey."

Dad also hugs me, and then they leave my hut.

I stand out on the deck and take in the view. I can't believe this is where I'll be sleeping for the next six nights. I've never been to such a beautiful place before, and I can't wait to explore more of Belize.

But first, I'm going to relax.

2

MONIQUE

"Seester!" Adeline runs toward me with her arms wide open and a huge smile. We wrap each other in a hug as soon as we meet. "It's so good to see you!"

"It's good to see you! It's been way too long!" The last time we saw each other was in May, when I flew home to the States for a couple of weeks.

As we release one another, I see Andre behind her. "Hi, Monique," he says, moving closer to give me a hug.

"It's good to see you, Andre," I say as we embrace.

"Mom and Dad are already in The Bistro," Adeline says. "They went a little early to make sure we got a big enough table."

"Let's go find them," I reply, and we start walking toward the restaurant.

It doesn't take long for us to walk across the sand to the entrance. We tell the hostess that our parents are already there, and she leads us to their table. I'm immediately impressed with the ambience of this place. There are no walls, just a railing separating the dining area from the beach, so every table has a seaside view.

"Hi!" Mom and Dad greet us, as does everyone else around the table.

We're the last ones to arrive. The Blakes are already here as well. Kyle looks the same as I remember, just older. But Kevin looks different. *Good* different.

Dan and Kathy stand to greet us. Kathy gives me a hug. As my mom's best friend, she was like an aunt to Adeline and me, and since she didn't have any daughters of her own, she often spoiled us with girly things. Whenever we saw her, she would always have something for us, whether it was hair accessories, nail polish, makeup, or even a cute outfit from time to time.

"It's so good to see you!" Kathy gushes. "I'm glad you could make the trip from Paris!"

"So am I. And it's great to see you again, too!"

"Have you seen Kevin and Kyle yet?" she asks, pointing toward her sons standing across the table from us. "I know it's been years since you've all seen each other. This is Kyle's fiancée, Sarah."

Sarah smiles and waves. She's almost as tall as Kyle, who's a little over six feet, and her dark brown hair has soft waves that go past her shoulders. Her skin is tan, her makeup is flawless, and she has long pink fingernails. "It's nice to meet you," she says.

"It's nice to meet you, too," I reply.

"It's good to see you, Monique," Kyle says with a crooked smile.

My first impression of adult Kyle is that he still comes across as a douchebag.

But I'm nice. "Wow, Kyle, it's been a long time!"

"It definitely has," he replies, eyeing me up and down. *Ick.*

I turn my attention to Kevin, who's standing quietly, which is typical Kevin. Always standing back from his brother and shy. But adult Kevin is something childhood Kevin was not—he's *hot. As. Sin.*

"Hi, Kevin," I say, and his lips lift in a smile.

"Monique," he says, stepping forward with his hand out for me to shake.

So formal. And so sexy.

I shake his hand, and time seems to stand still. Warmth spreads throughout my body as tingles settle in my belly. I never expected to have *this* sort of reaction to Kevin Blake. *Kevin.* The boy who helped his brother torture me—and Adeline—whenever our families visited each other when we were kids. Chased us. Pulled our hair. Tried to tickle us, spy on us, and tease us mercilessly. Of course, Kyle did the bulk of it while Kevin was just his accomplice, but still. Since when am I attracted to Kevin Blake?

"Let's all have a seat!" Dad's voice pulls me back to the here and now.

Everyone sits around the table, and I end up directly across from Kevin. Adeline is to my right, and no one is to my left since I'm on the end.

"How many years has it been?" Kevin asks, lifting a bottle of Belikin beer to his lips, his eyes on me.

I cock an eyebrow as I consider the answer. "It's been at

least a decade," I reply, trying to remember the last time we saw each other. "I remember going to your graduation party, and you and your family came to mine, but was that the last time?"

That seems so long ago. I've seen his parents a couple of times over the years, but not him or Kyle. When I found out they were all joining my family on this Belize vacation, I wondered what it would be like to see them again, especially in a tropical location.

"I think you're right," Kevin says. "It must've been right after we graduated. Those are my last memories of seeing you, too."

"So tell me what you've been doing all these years," I say, curious as to what he does, where he lives... if he's single...

"Where should I start?" Kevin chuckles. "After high school, I went to Columbia River University up near Portland, Oregon, and studied computer science. After graduating, I interned with a Portland company before I was lucky enough to get hired at a tech company in Seattle. I still work there and love my job, especially since I can work from home."

"That's awesome. Do you enjoy living in Seattle? One of my employees grew up there and says it's a beautiful city." Becca has invited me to visit Seattle with her some day, but I don't know who I'd trust to run my shop if we both left Paris at the same time. I'm not sure if any of my part-time employees could handle it without Becca or me there to help.

"I do. It's a great city." He cracks a smile, and I get that tingle in my belly again. Kevin is having a real effect on me.

"Do you miss Southern California at all?"

He shrugs a shoulder. "Sometimes I do, but I've grown to love the Pacific Northwest. How about you? Are you still living in Paris?"

I nod. "I am. My store is doing well, and I absolutely love it there."

"That's awesome. Mom has told me about your shop. Congratulations," he says sincerely.

"Thank you," I reply. "And same to you."

The server arrives at our table to take our drink orders, pulling my attention away from Kevin. I quickly look at the menu as everyone else places their orders, and by the time the server gets to me, I've made my decision. I order a piña colada, and Kevin orders another Belikin. After our server walks away, everyone at our table continues talking again, including Kevin and me.

He inquires about my shop and living in Paris, and I ask about his job and living in Seattle. We engage with everyone else at the table throughout dinner, but Kevin and I spend a good portion of the evening getting reacquainted with one another. I like grown-up Kevin, and not just because I'm attracted to him. He seems smart and down-to-earth, and he's easy to talk to.

After our delicious dinner, everyone—my parents, Adeline, Andre, and the Blakes—all decide to take a walk on the beach. It's a gorgeous evening. Somehow, Kevin and I end up walking behind everyone else, giving us the opportunity to continue our conversation.

"This place is incredible," he says as we walk along the sandy shore. "I've never been anywhere like this."

"Neither have I. The fact that our hotel is right here on this beach, just feet away from the water, is pretty amazing."

"Where's your hotel room?" Kevin asks.

I look up toward the buildings, and we happen to be walking right past my little hut. "That's it right there," I say, pointing at my room.

"No way," Kevin says. "We're neighbors. I'm in the hut next to you."

I suddenly remember that Mom mentioned that to me earlier. "It's a nice room. I can't believe I can see the beach right outside my door."

"I know," Kevin agrees. "I bet the sunrises are beautiful."

That thought hadn't occurred to me. "I bet they are. I wonder if I'll ever wake up early enough to see one."

"I hope to," he says. "I usually wake up early anyway."

Suddenly, Kyle, who's walking just in front of us with Sarah, turns around, continuing to walk backward. "This guy never sleeps in," he says, cutting into our conversation. "Even as a kid, he would wake up early. It drove me fucking crazy." He laughs, and I realize Kyle is anything but sober.

"Yeah, yeah," Kevin says, placating his older brother.

Suddenly, Kyle loses his footing in the uneven sand. "Shit!" he says, falling backward and landing hard on the ground.

"Oh no, baby!" Sarah puts her hands out to him. I

doubt she could help him up, though. She's thin and doesn't appear to have the strength to lift him off the ground.

As everyone else in our group turns around to see what happened, Kyle's head falls back in laughter. I notice his parents shake their heads, and I sense their son's antics do not amuse them.

"Are you okay?" Andre asks, offering him a hand.

"Fuck yeah, man," Kyle says, taking Andre's hand and allowing him to help him stand.

Kathy rolls her eyes. "Watch your language," she tells her son.

"Sorry, Mom," Kyle says, dusting the sand off his clothes. His apology sounds anything but sincere. Then he looks at Sarah. "Are you ready to go back to the room?"

She nods. "Yeah, I'm tired."

Kyle and Sarah say good night to everyone and head to their room. The rest of us continue our walk, and Kevin and I continue our conversation.

By the time everyone else agrees it's time to walk back to our rooms for the night, I've learned all sorts of things about Kevin's life, including the fact he's currently single. I have to admit I'm developing a crush on my childhood friend.

This could be bad. Our parents are best friends. I've known Kevin my entire life. Things could get complicated *real* fast.

But it's just a crush. A crush doesn't have to mean anything. Kevin doesn't have to find out, and it's probably best he never does. I can enjoy this vacation with him and our families without anyone ever knowing. That's how it *has* to be. I can't imagine how awkward things would get if my feelings were made known.

"Good night," Mom says as I give her a hug.

"Sleep good. See you in the morning," I reply before saying good night to everyone else.

Everyone except Kevin, since we still need to walk a little farther to get to our huts.

"Well, tomorrow should be fun," he says as we walk.

"Yeah, I love snorkeling. Have you ever gone before?"

"Once in Hawaii," he replies. "But that was when I was thirteen, so it's been a while." He laughs.

"I haven't been in a few years either, but it should be pretty easy. Like riding a bike." At least, I hope it is.

"True," Kevin agrees as we approach our huts. "Well, I guess I'll see you in the morning. It was nice talking with you, Monique. It's great to see you again after all these years."

I smile. "It's been nice talking with you, too, Kevin," I reply, hoping I'm not giving him flirty vibes.

But, at the same time, part of me hopes I *am* giving off flirty vibes.

No—nothing can happen between Kevin and me!

"Good night," he says with a little wave as he walks toward his hut.

"Good night," I reply, then turn toward my own.

Whew! What a first day in Belize.

3

KEVIN

Whew. What a first day in Belize.

I was not looking forward to this trip. Spending a whole week with my brother and his fiancée is not my idea of fun. But I knew how important it was to Mom to have the whole family together for Thanksgiving, and I didn't want to crush her dreams of having a family vacation with all of us in Belize. I also knew having the Blanchets here would create more of a buffer between my brother and me, so I agreed to come along. Still, this isn't a vacation I was counting down to.

Things seemed to turn up at dinner, though. It's been a decade since I last saw Monique, and I was pleasantly surprised at how well we got along tonight. We weren't what anyone would consider close friends as kids even though our families spent plenty of time together. Kyle was always, well, Kyle... not exactly the nicest guy on the planet... and I was the dumb younger brother trying to be cool like him. Unfortunately, that meant I wasn't always nice to Monique and Adeline. Kyle and I would chase them, tease them, and annoy the shit out of them. As we got older, I stopped doing those things, but I was an awkward, quiet teen who kept to myself, not interacting with the girls much.

Any girls, for that matter.

Sure, I was attracted to girls—including Monique. Adeline's younger, so I was never interested in her in that way, but I did have a crush on Monique. I didn't know how to act cool around girls, though. Everyone knew me as Kyle's younger brother, and Kyle didn't exactly have the best reputation. I didn't want to follow in his footsteps, so I laid low.

Honestly, I was much too shy and insecure back then. And that shyness even extended to Monique and Adeline even though I'd known them my entire life.

Once I moved over a thousand miles north to attend college, though, I was able to break free from being "Kyle's younger brother." Nobody at Columbia River University knew who the hell Kyle Blake was since he didn't go to school there. I was finally able to come out of my shell and be myself without anyone pre-judging me. College was where I came into my own and matured, and where I started working out... which eventually led to girls noticing me, and my dating life finally began.

I dated a lot of girls in college. I had one long-term relationship that lasted through my junior and senior years, but she took a job back in her hometown in Eastern Washington after we graduated. The distance between us became too difficult, so we broke up. I've dated girls here and there over the years, but nothing too serious has materialized since then.

I fell in love with the Pacific Northwest and vowed never to return to Southern California. Although I love my parents and where I grew up, I didn't want to live near Kyle. He may be my brother, but I'll be the first to admit he's a certified douchebag. I don't know how he turned out that way since my parents are the nicest people on the planet. He's the black sheep of the family, for sure. I think he was easily influenced by the friends he made growing up, and that's how he turned out the way he did, unfortunately.

Monique's beautiful face pops in my head as I lie in my bed, listening to the waves of the Caribbean Sea lapping against the shore. I enjoyed talking with her all through dinner and during our walk on the beach. Since we're the only two single people on this joint family vacation, I suppose we may end up hanging out together more, and I'm perfectly okay with that. Not only is Monique a beautiful woman, she's kind and nice to talk to. Although we live totally different lives on completely separate continents, we found we have a lot in common. Snorkeling tomorrow should be fun.

This is the first time I've had a positive thought about this vacation, so that's a definite plus.

"This is fucking incredible!" Kyle's crass comment is heard by everyone on the boat, including the other two people not in our party who happened to book the same excursion.

Mom looks mortified that her son would say such a thing in a public place, and I empathize with her. After all, I'm mortified by most of the things Kyle does.

However, Kyle's right—this place *is* fucking incredible! As the tour company employees drop anchor, I look around at the view. We're literally in the middle of the Caribbean, with a small sandy island a few yards away from us that we're going to snorkel around today. This island can't be more than thirty feet long. It's like a sandbar in the Caribbean Sea, with a couple of picnic tables, four or five palm trees, and an outhouse sitting atop it. Turquoise blue water surrounds the island, and as I look down from the boat I can see fish swimming about.

"Welcome to Silk Caye," one of the employees says in his Belize accent. "When you exit the boat, you will swim the short distance to the shallow water where you can stand and walk up to the shore. We will hand out all of the snorkeling gear once everyone is on the island."

I look at Monique, sitting next to me. "This is going to be amazing."

She nods in agreement. "This is already spectacular. I didn't know anywhere on earth like this existed."

Everyone exits the boat and heads toward the shore. Monique jumps into the water, then it's my turn. We make our way up to the small island along with everyone else. The hour-long boat ride to get here gave us great views, but this—I really have no words for this. It's truly a little slice of heaven in the middle of the Caribbean.

"Oh my gosh!" Sarah squeals a few feet away, standing on the other side of a picnic table, pointing down at something on the sand. "Little crabs!"

I step closer to take a look, and sure enough, several small crabs scurry along the sand.

"You should pick one up," Kyle says. "I dare you."

Jesus. Why is my brother such a moron?

Before anyone can tell her it's not the best idea, Sarah bends down and picks up one of the tiny crabs. Before she can stand again, she shrieks, shaking her hand, trying to get the little guy to release her.

Kyle doubles over in laughter.

"Ow, ow, ow!" The little crab finally lets go of her and scrambles away on the sand. Sarah stands and hits Kyle on the arm. "Don't laugh at me!"

"Oh, come on," Kyle says. "That was funny!"

Sarah shakes her hand, obviously still in pain. "No, it wasn't."

Mom walks over to the scene. "Kyle, you should know better," she scolds him as if he's a child. Then she carefully takes Sarah's hand to look at the damage. "I think you'll be okay. It didn't break the skin."

I turn toward Monique, who subtly rolls her eyes at me.

"What's going on?" Adeline says as she and her boyfriend walk up to join us.

"Oh, nothing. Sarah picked up a crab, and it pinched her."

"Ouch," Adeline says. "That's why you don't pick up crabs."

Monique and I both laugh at her comment before we're interrupted by the snorkeling employees as they give us instructions for receiving our gear. Everyone lines up as they tell us to do, and it doesn't take long to pass everything out. After explaining a few other things, the employees lead us out into the water again.

"I hope we see lots of cool fish," Monique says.

"I'm sure we will," I reply. "I already saw a few when we were still on the boat."

We follow them to where the water is deeper, then begin swimming and snorkeling our way around the island.

As soon as I put my head in the water, I'm in awe. I see all kinds of fish as we begin swimming. Sea life of different sizes and colors, and even practically translucent jellyfish swim all around. Our guide informs us that these small jellyfish don't sting, though, so we don't need to worry.

We make our way around the entire island in about a half hour, then we take a break for lunch. Some of the other tour guide employees stayed on shore to prepare lunch while we snorkeled, and as soon as everyone is out of the water, we grab plates and dish up the chicken, macaroni salad, and rolls they provided.

After filling my plate, I look for a place to sit. Luckily, I find an empty seat next to Monique at one of the picnic tables. She's sitting with Adeline and her boyfriend, so I decide to join them.

"Do you mind if I sit here?" I ask.

Monique looks up at me, adjusting her sunglasses. "Sure... I mean, you're welcome to join us."

I sit next to her and look across at Adeline and Andre. "That was a pretty cool snorkeling experience."

"Yeah, it was," Andre says. "I've gone snorkeling in Mexico before, but it was nothing like that."

"I'm glad we get to go out again after lunch," Adeline agrees.

The four of us continue talking as we eat. Andre is a good guy, and he and Adeline seem happy. Unlike Kyle and Sarah, who seem to have more drama between them than any other couple I know.

I look around and enjoy the view. A couple of pelican-like birds sit on palm tree branches, watching the water carefully for their next meal. This has to be one of the most beautiful places on earth, and I feel fortunate to be here. I suddenly feel bad for my pessimistic attitude toward this trip before.

After lunch, we all head out into the water again. This time, the guide swims in the opposite direction around the island. Once again, I'm awestruck by the underwater beauty. Monique swims next to me and points at a fish that appears to sparkle. It's beautiful, and luckily, our guide is nearby. He notices us looking at the fish, and as soon as the fish is gone, he motions for us to go above water. "It's a parrotfish," he says.

"That was awesome," I gush. "I've never seen anything like that before."

"It was so colorful and sparkly," Monique says in amazement.

We both put our snorkel mouthpieces back in, then go back underwater, and it's not long before we see another incredible sight that the rest of our group happens to see as well. We all watch as a large fish, about four feet long, swims right under all of us. Our guide once again motions for everyone to go to the surface after it passes. "That was a permit fish," he explains.

Monique and I look at each other, amazed once more. "I can't believe how cool this is," she says before putting her mouthpiece in and going underwater again.

"Neither can I," I mutter before going back under myself.

Our snorkeling adventure continues to be an unbelievable experience. Once we finish, we all load up on the boat again, and the guides take us to an area known for nurse sharks and turtle sightings, and we're not disappointed. We see several of them swimming around the boat, and it's quite a sight. Everyone stands around the boat's perimeter, looking over the railing at the beautiful sea life. The guides won't allow us to get in the water, though, and it's *not* because of the nurse sharks. They're harmless. The turtles are the ones who get aggressive and bite.

As the boat takes us back to Placencia, Monique and I sit beside each other. We're both tired after being in the sun and snorkeling all afternoon, so we don't talk much. Before I know it, she nods off, and her head ends up on my shoulder. I try to stay as still as possible so I don't disturb her.

Of course, Kyle has to be the first one to notice.

"Aw, isn't that sweet," he says sarcastically.

Sarah nudges him. "Stop it. She just fell asleep on

him." She rolls her eyes. Sarah's clearly annoyed with him at the moment.

Kyle turns to face her. "What? I can say what I want to my brother. I'm just joking."

Sarah doesn't say anything. She just rolls her eyes again.

"Okay. Whatever." Kyle rolls his eyes as well, then turns away from her. Although they sit beside each other, his back is to her now.

I stay quiet, not wanting to encourage Kyle. I look at my parents, occupying the other end of the boat with Monique's parents. They're oblivious to everything here. I also see Adeline and Andre, who both look tired. Adeline's head rests on his shoulder like Monique's is on mine. We're all tired, and that's probably the reason Kyle's being a dick right now.

Or at least it's perpetuating his bad attitude right now.

Luckily, he doesn't make any other smart-ass comments to me or anyone else the rest of the boat ride back.

4

MONIQUE

I wake suddenly, and it takes me a moment to realize where I am. I'm on a boat. It's getting tied up to a dock. And my cheek is resting on someone's shoulder.

Startled, I lift my head to see who's acted as my pillow for the boat ride.

Kevin's eyes meet mine, and he smiles. "Hey, Sleeping Beauty."

Embarrassed, I smile sheepishly. "Sorry. I didn't mean to fall asleep on you."

"It was no problem. Really." Kevin stands, and I realize everyone else is gathering their personal belongings to get off the boat.

I'm not sure what else to say, so I do the same and make sure I have everything I brought with me. My phone, wallet, and towel are all accounted for, so I sling my backpack over my shoulder and get up to exit the boat.

I can't believe I fell asleep, but at the same time I can.

I'm exhausted. After spending the past couple of days traveling, not fully adjusted to the jet lag, and snorkeling all afternoon, I needed that nap. I'm grateful Kevin let me rest on his shoulder.

Dad drives our family back to the hotel, and the Blakes are in another SUV they rented. I'm in the back next to Adeline, who's sitting in the middle between Andre and me. Everyone's quiet on the ride back, probably because we're all so tired. It was a long and quite adventurous day out on the water. I've never experienced anything like that before—being on Silk Caye, a small island in the middle of the sea, seeing so many tropical fish, the big permit fish that swam beneath us, and all of the nurse sharks and turtles we saw from the boat before heading back to shore. Incredible.

Kevin was nice to hang around, too... and nice to look at as well. He obviously hits the gym on a regular basis. I was surprised when he took his shirt off and revealed his firm six-pack. Teenage Kevin was not in this good of shape. I'd be lying if I said I didn't have butterflies around him all day.

He's definitely my type, but he's also the son of my parents' best friends. Honestly, it's strange to think I'm finding Kevin so attractive after last night and today. Maybe I'm more exhausted than I realize, and it's affecting my hormones.

Once we get back to the hotel, the Blakes park next to our car. When Kevin gets out of their SUV, he stretches his arms above his head, causing his shirt to lift a little, revealing his lower torso and those muscles that make a V shape... and *damn*... that feeling I've had around him comes back again.

Why do I have to be so attracted to him?

Thankfully, everyone agrees to rest for an hour before meeting at The Bistro for dinner. I could use a little more time to rest. After I return to my hut, I change into a T-shirt and pajama shorts, set my alarm to wake me in forty-five minutes, and lie down for a nap.

I can't get Kevin out of my head, though. I close my eyes, and his handsome face is still there. The day's events replay in my mind like a movie, and I remember how much fun we had snorkeling together. I like him. I mean, of course I like him—I've known him my entire life. His mom is like my aunt, though, which makes him like my cousin. *Ew.* No. I can't find my cousin attractive.

But he's not really my cousin...

My alarm wakes me, and I roll over to turn it off. Thankfully, I finally managed to doze off and get a little shut-eye. As short as the nap was, though, I do feel rejuvenated. And hungry. I'm glad we're meeting for dinner soon.

I get undressed and pull on a comfortable sundress, then brush my hair and make myself presentable for dinner. After I spritz on a little perfume and slide my flip-flops onto my feet, I grab my purse and leave for The Bistro.

Kevin walks out of his hut at the same time.

"Hey," he says, walking toward me.

He's like my cousin, he's like my cousin... I try saying that mantra in my head as I lock my hut's door, but I don't think it's working.

As soon as I turn and see Kevin waiting for me, all I can think is how fucking hot he is. He is *not* my cousin, and I can't deny that Kevin Blake has grown up to be a gorgeous, sexy man.

"Hey," I say, and we begin walking toward The Bistro together.

"I took a quick nap. I was wiped out after today."

"Me, too." There's a slight breeze, and I get a whiff of his cologne. The scent must have an effect on my pheromones because it makes me even more attracted to him.

"Your jet lag must be bad, coming all the way from Paris," he says as we approach The Bistro's entrance. "I can't imagine how tired you must be."

I shrug. "Yeah, I'm exhausted, but I think I'll be all right."

We walk into the restaurant and immediately see our parents already seated at a large table. We walk over to join them. Adeline and Andre arrive shortly after us, then Kyle and Sarah. They seem to be in some sort of argument with each other, not talking much. I'm fine with that, though, since most of what comes out of Kyle's mouth is annoying.

Dinner is good. The shrimp tacos I ordered are delicious, as well as the margarita. I've decided The Bistro is one of the best restaurants I've ever eaten at before... and I live in Paris, one of the culinary meccas of the world.

Kevin and I talk throughout dinner, sharing fond memories from our childhoods. We interact with everyone else at the table, but we find ourselves talking just between the two of us more while everyone else discusses other things. We tell each other stories about our college years. Like last night, the more I learn about Kevin's life, the more I like him.

By the time everyone's ready to leave, I realize my crush on Kevin is undeniable. Yeah, it's weird to think of him this way, but it's just a crush. Nothing has to happen between us... I can just fantasize about him later. I'm not going to feel weird or guilty about it, though. Kevin is like the man of my dreams, both in personality and how he looks.

Unlike last night, everyone's too tired to walk on the beach after we leave The Bistro. Everyone says good night and heads back to their rooms. Kevin's the last one I say good night to since his hut is beside mine. As we both stand on our porches, unlocking our doors, he says, "Sleep good, Monique. See you in the morning."

I turn and smile at him. "You, too. Good night." I give him a little wave as I open my door and go inside.

My heart pitter-patters, thinking of Kevin's adorable face, wondering what adventures tomorrow will bring.

I pour myself a cup of coffee. I slept well last night, and I slept in for once. I feel refreshed. Today is Thanksgiving back in the US. Aside from having dinner all together tonight to celebrate, it's going to be a chill day for everyone to do their own thing, and I don't have anything planned. The only thing I want to do is enjoy the beach here at the hotel. Maybe I'll read a book. Maybe I'll sketch some new designs I have in mind.

In an attempt to save some of my spending money, I decided to put the coffee maker in my room to work instead of going to The Bistro for breakfast. The hotel provided coffee, as well as sugar and creamer packets in the small kitchenette, so I'm set.

I decide to do something I haven't had a chance to do yet—sit on my hut's front porch and enjoy the view of the Caribbean Sea. As I open the door and step outside, I take a deep breath. This view is absolutely stunning. I've slept the past two nights with the windows open so I could fall asleep to the sound of the waves. It helps me relax, and it's a reminder of how lucky I am to be here in Belize.

I sit on one of the chairs on the porch and take a sip of my coffee. This is perfect. This is what vacation is all about. Yesterday, snorkeling was amazing, but there's something about having nothing on the agenda and a beautiful view to enjoy. I let my head fall back against the chair and close my eyes, enjoying the tranquility of this place.

"Happy Thanksgiving." Kevin's deep, sexy voice makes my eyes pop open.

I lift my head and turn toward his hut. He's sitting on his porch, doing the same thing I am.

He lifts his mug in cheers, then lowers it again. "You can't beat this view." He takes a sip of whatever's in his cup.

Lucky mug. Kevin looks sexy, his hair a little messy as if he hasn't combed through it since waking up. I run my hand through my own hair, hoping I don't look like a sloppy mess. It's still wet from the shower I took before making my coffee.

"Yeah, I can't complain," I reply. "The coffee is pretty good for hotel coffee, too."

Kevin nods in agreement, then takes another sip. "It's so peaceful here. Maybe I should relocate so I can enjoy this every morning."

I laugh. "I wish that was possible. It would be amazing to wake up to this view every day. I'm not sure my boutique would be as successful here as it is in Paris, though."

"Sucks for you. Lucky for me, I can do my job from anywhere," Kevin says, lifting his laptop for me to see. I didn't notice it before.

"You're working?" I ask, surprised.

He nods. "Yeah, there were some things I had to get done. I just finished, though."

"That's good," I reply.

"Anyway, I think I'll stop by the local real estate office today and find a place." He winks to let me know he's joking.

I laugh again. "Yeah, okay. Sounds like a plan."

"I'll make sure to get a big enough place so you can visit me," he says with a sexy smile that makes my belly muscles clench.

"I appreciate that," I reply. "If you could find a place with a guesthouse similar to this hut, I'd be happy."

"I'll see what I can do." Kevin chuckles.

We both take sips of our coffee, and I look out at the view again. The beach is empty, except for one Belizean woman near The Bistro who has a blanket full of hand-made goods she's selling. I noticed a few people on the beach like this yesterday, selling their stuff to tourists. I wonder how much money they actually make from selling bracelets, little wooden bowls, baskets, and other souvenir trinkets. It must be enough to live off if they continue doing it.

"Want to kayak?"

Kevin's question steals my attention, and I turn to face him again. "What?" Did he just ask me if I wanted to kayak?

He points toward a few kayaks leaning against a palm tree. "They're for hotel guests to borrow. We just have to ask, and they'll give us paddles to use. Wanna go?"

I look at the kayaks, then back at him. The fact that he wants to spend time with me is a bit thrilling. I can spend time up close and personal with Kevin while paddling a kayak around the Caribbean. Why wouldn't I say yes?

"When do you want to go?" I ask, abandoning my plans of a chill day relaxing on the beach.

Kevin's smile widens. He seems happy that I agreed to join him. "Whenever you want. It can be later. I'm not doing anything else today, except for our Belizean-style Thanksgiving dinner later."

I smile. "Gimme twenty minutes to get ready, and I'll meet you at the kayaks."

"Sounds like a plan."

Carrying my cup of coffee, I head inside to get ready. Kevin and I are going to hang out. Sure, we spent all day together yesterday, as well as the evening before, but it'll just be the two of us this time. I have butterflies just thinking about it.

Twenty minutes later, I leave my hut and find Kevin by the kayaks. He's standing with two paddles in his hands, and he smiles as I approach him.

"I got the paddles for us already," he says. "Do you want to go in a tandem kayak, or one by yourself?"

I consider his question. Being in a tandem kayak together would make it easier for us to talk while we paddle around. If we're in our own kayaks, I'll be by myself. "Let's do a tandem one."

He smiles, seemingly happy with my choice. "Perfect."

After choosing one of the tandem kayaks, we each grab an end and walk it out to the water.

"Have you ever kayaked before?" he asks as we get onto the boat.

From the front seat, I turn around to answer him. "Yes, I have. Once." I turn back around and grab my paddle.

"Cool. So have I. Once." We push off from shore and begin paddling out into the open water.

The water is clear, although not as clear as at Silk Caye yesterday. I wonder if we'll see any fish as we paddle around.

"Where did you kayak before?" he asks.

"Oh, this lake outside of Paris. It was a couple of years ago." I don't want to go into the details of that kayaking trip. I was with a guy I was dating at the time. "What about you?"

"It was last summer on a lake near Seattle. It was pretty

fun. I considered buying my own kayak afterward, but I never did."

"Really? You must've really enjoyed it."

He chuckles. "Yeah, it was all right. I'm glad I didn't spend the money on buying one, though, since I'm not really *that* into it. I was dating a girl at the time who loved kayaking."

Oh.

Screw it. I'll tell him how my last kayaking adventure was with a guy I was dating, too. "That's funny. I was also on a date when I went kayaking before."

He laughs. "Is that right? What a coincidence."

Just then, I see a fish jump out of the water not too far in front of me. "Oh my gosh! Did you see that?"

"What? No. What was it?"

I stop paddling. "A fish," I say, pointing to where I saw it.

Suddenly, another fish jumps.

"Did you see that?" Kevin asks with excitement.

I nod. "Yeah, I did!"

We sit here for a moment on the calm water, waiting to see if another fish jumps. Nothing else happens, though, so I turn my attention to the water next to the boat. Before I know it, I see a couple of jellyfish swimming beside us. "Look, look, look!" I can't contain my excitement as I point at the jellyfish in the water.

"Whoa! This is so cool."

Kevin and I watch the jellyfish until they disappear out of sight. "Shall we continue paddling?" I ask.

"Let's go," he says, and we both pick up our paddles and continue on our way.

Kevin and I kayak for quite a while, enjoying the scenery and the wildlife. We stop to watch fish swimming or jumping out of the water whenever we notice them. I thoroughly enjoy myself, and although it's a workout, I also find the activity relaxing.

When we return to our hotel, Kevin and I carry the kayak back to where we got it from. "That was a lot of fun," he says. "Thanks for going with me."

"I had fun, too. Thanks for inviting me."

"Here"—he reaches for my paddle—"I'll return these."

"Thanks," I reply, handing mine to him.

"Are you hungry?" he asks.

"Now that I think about it, I am pretty hungry." I suppose all that paddling worked up an appetite.

"Would you like to grab a bite with me?"

Yes. I've enjoyed my time with Kevin so far today, and I don't want to say goodbye to him yet. "Sure. At The Bistro?"

He smiles, seeming happy I accepted his offer, which lights me up inside. "Actually, I saw a bowling alley down the street. Do you like to bowl? I'm sure they have food, too."

I remember seeing the small bowling alley when we drove back from snorkeling yesterday. It's within walking distance of the hotel. "That sounds great," I reply. "I just need to grab my purse."

"Okay. I'll return the paddles, so meet me by the hotel's front desk."

I agree to his plan, then head toward my hut. I can't remember the last time I went bowling, but I have a feeling I'll have a good time with Kevin. Kayaking with him was fun. Snorkeling with him was fun. Dinners with him the past couple of nights were fun. One thing's for sure—Kevin and I have a good time together.

5

KEVIN

"Woohoo! Did you see that?" Monique gloats as she walks toward me after taking her last shot of the game.

Her bowling skills have shocked me. "Another strike? You kicked my ass!"

She laughs, then sits in the seat next to me. "I can't believe it! I haven't bowled in years."

I shake my head, pretending to be disappointed about losing the game. "Do you want to play again?"

"Sure," Monique replies, then pops a fry in her mouth.

I reset the computer for a new game. Today has been a lot of fun with Monique. I enjoy spending time with her. We have a good time together, we get along well, and she's beautiful. I can't deny that I'm crushing hard on my child-hood friend. Again.

The computer restarts our game, and the pins get put in place. With only four lanes, this is the smallest bowling alley I've ever been to. Two other lanes are being used, so we're not the only people here right now. The food is pretty good, too. We ordered nachos, chicken fingers, and fries to share. I've been drinking Belikin beer, which is the most popular beer in Belize, and Monique ordered a margarita.

It's my turn first, so I reach for a ball. I glance at Monique, who's breaking a chicken finger in half. She's beautiful. It may be risky, but I wouldn't mind taking things to the next level with her. Wouldn't that be crazy? Our parents are best friends and we've known each other since birth. That would be weird… right?

I can't help myself, though. "Do you want to make this game interesting?" I ask, hoping she goes along with what I'm going to propose.

Monique cocks an eyebrow. "What do you have in mind?"

Yes.

"If I win, you have to agree to get a drink with me at The Bistro when we get back."

Her eyebrows shoot up in surprise. "*That's* what you want if you win?" she asks. "You just want to spend more time with me?"

I nod. "Yeah, I do."

We hold each other's gaze for a moment, and I notice she's blushing. *Good.* That means I'm having an effect on her.

"W-well, what if *I* win?" she asks.

I shrug a shoulder. "What do you want if you win?"

She puts her forefinger on her chin and looks up as if she's contemplating the answer to that. *God, she's adorable.*

She puts her hand down and looks at me again, a mischievous look on her face. "If *I* win, you have to play truth or dare with me."

Her proposal takes me by surprise. "Truth or dare?"

She nods slowly. The way she's looking at me right now is a total turn-on, and suddenly, I want to throw the game and lose so I can play truth or dare with her.

"Okay. Deal," I say, putting my hand out for her to shake.

She gives me a wickedly sexy smile, then shakes my hand. "Deal."

Let the game begin.

"I am the bowling champ!"

Monique and I walk along the street, heading back to the hotel. We had a great time and shared a lot of laughs as we played that last high-stakes game. Luckily, I didn't have to try hard to lose, though. Monique truly is a lot better than me at bowling.

And I'm glad she won.

"Yes, yes, you are," I say with a laugh. "I'll have a trophy made for you."

"Will you engrave my name on it?"

"Yes, of course. It'll say 'Monique Blanchet, Bowling Champion of Belize, Number One in the World.'"

"Aw, yes!" She laughs. "Number one in the world, and number one in your heart."

You have no idea.

I laugh with her. "For sure."

I can only hope this game of truth or dare pays off for me in the end. I'm hoping to at least get a kiss out of it. Maybe more. My feelings for Monique are growing, and I feel like a horny teenager again.

We cross the street to our hotel, and to our surprise, the SUV my parents rented pulls into the parking lot. Sarah is driving, and Kyle's in the passenger seat. They get out of the car just as we approach, and Kyle sees us right away.

I can already tell he's been drinking. That must be why Sarah drove.

"Hey, little brother!" He stumbles a bit as he closes the passenger-side door. "Where did you two go?" He waves his finger at Monique and me.

"We went bowling," I reply.

Sarah walks around the car. She doesn't look happy. "Hey," she says before gently taking Kyle's arm. "Come on, babe, let's get back to the room."

Kyle scowls at his fiancée. "What? No. We're going to the bar with Kevin and Monique here."

Shit. He's going to be difficult, I just know it. And by the look on Sarah's face, I'm guessing he already has been.

"No, no more drinking right now," she says. "Let's go rest for a bit."

Kyle shakes his arm out of her loose grip. "No. I don't want to go rest."

I look at Sarah, who looks at me. "He got kicked out of the bar we were at in town," she explains, looking exasperated.

"Hey! They were dicks there!" Kyle says, his voice getting louder.

I know he needs to get back to his room, and I need to help Sarah get him there.

"Come on, man," I say in a gentle tone. "Let's all go to your room and hang out for a bit."

Kyle glares at me for a moment. "You guys want to hang out?"

"Yeah," I say, carefully patting him on the shoulder. "Let's go."

"Okay, but I want a beer."

"I'll get us beers from the bar and meet you at your room," I offer, hoping he agrees.

We all start walking. "Okay, fine. Get me a Belikin," he says.

Thank goodness. I can tell he'll make a scene if he's out in public right now, and that can't happen. Who knows what he might do here if he got kicked out of a bar in town? The last thing I want is for Kyle to make an ass of himself at the hotel we're staying at. Mom and Dad would be so embarrassed.

"Sarah, do you want anything?" I ask.

"Just a Coke," she says, then follows it up with, "please."

I can tell she's embarrassed. I am, too. "We'll meet you at your room in a bit," I say to her and Kyle as they walk toward the hotel, and Monique and I walk toward the bar at The Bistro.

"How did your brother turn out to be such an ass?" Monique asks.

"I honestly don't know. I hate that he acts the way he does."

"Sorry," she apologizes. "I mean, your parents are some of the nicest people I know, and you're nothing like Kyle either. He was even mean when we were kids."

We reach the bar, and I lean against it. "I don't know. I wish he wasn't like this."

I get the bartender's attention, and he comes over to take our order. Although I know the last thing my brother needs right now is another drink, I order him a Belikin like he requested. If I don't, he'll likely come to the bar himself and end up causing a scene.

"Is he an alcoholic?" Monique asks as we wait for the drinks.

I scoff. "You could say that. As far as I know, he doesn't drink *all* the time, but when he does drink, he doesn't handle it well."

She nods but doesn't say anything else. I'm sure she doesn't know what to say. It's a difficult situation. I'm at a loss with my brother, and I don't even see him that often anymore.

The bartender returns with a Belikin and three Cokes. Monique and I settled on a nonalcoholic choice, figuring it's probably the safest bet.

Speaking of bets... Damn. Leave it to Kyle to ruin the fun Monique and I were having. Who knows if we'll actually follow through on the truth or dare game now that we have to deal with my idiot brother.

Monique carries two of the Cokes, while I carry the other one and the Belikin. We make our way over to Kyle and Sarah's hotel room, and I knock on the door. It doesn't take long before Sarah opens it. "Hey," she says, letting us in.

"Hi." I hand her the Coke, then notice Kyle is asleep on the bed. "He passed out?"

"Yeah," she says with a sigh. "Thank goodness. I didn't want to deal with his drunk ass anymore."

I nod. "I understand. Are you okay?"

"Yeah," she replies, although I'm not convinced.

"What happened?" Monique asks. "I mean, at the bar where you were."

Sarah sits on the couch, so Monique and I sit on the two chairs available. I look at the beer in my hand, then take a sip. Why not? Kyle won't be drinking it.

"We decided to go into Placencia," Sarah explains. "Your parents let us use the SUV, so we drove to town and explored a bit. We walked around and went to some shops. Then we ended up at a bar for lunch. He started drinking, and before I knew it, he was drunk. He started playing pool with some other guys, but he started acting like a jerk since he was drunk. The bartender kicked him out. He even threatened to call the cops if he didn't leave. It was ridiculous."

I'm honestly not sure what she means by ridiculous— how they kicked Kyle out of the bar or how Kyle acted.

"Sorry you had to deal with that," Monique says before I have a chance to say anything.

Kyle snores, and I know he'll be out for a while. I look at my watch, and it's only four o'clock. I wonder if he'll stay out the entire night.

"Thanks for the Coke," Sarah says before taking a sip.

"No problem," I reply.

"I think I'll take a nap," she says, which I take as her subtle way of asking Monique and me to leave.

"Okay, cool. Will we see you at dinner with everyone later?" I stand, and so does Monique.

"Yeah... if I'm not asleep," Sarah says.

"Let us know if you need anything," I offer as Monique and I head for the door. "Do you have my number?"

Sarah nods. "Yeah, I do. Thanks."

Monique and I say goodbye, then leave. As we walk away from their hotel room, neither of us says anything. This whole situation has put a damper on the good time we were having a short time ago. I'm glad my parents weren't around to witness Kyle being a dumbass, but I wish I didn't have to deal with him.

"Well, that sucked," Monique says as we walk toward our huts.

"Yeah, it did." I take another drink of the beer in my hand. Then I notice Monique is still carrying two Cokes. We have an extra since I'm drinking Kyle's beer. "Let me carry one of those for you."

"Oh, it's not a problem," she says, but I still take it from her. "Thanks."

As we approach my hut, we stop walking. "What do you want to do now?" she asks, and I'm suddenly filled with a little hope. Hope that Kyle didn't completely ruin our fun day together.

"I don't know. Do you have anything in mind?"

Her lips curl up into a devilish grin. "I believe you owe me a game of truth or dare."

Yes! This is exactly what I was hoping for.

I smile. "That is true. Where do you want to play?"

She looks up and down the beach before shrugging. "Wanna go inside one of our huts?"

"Sure," I reply. "Let's go to yours."

She smiles, then leads the way to her hut.

As we walk in, I notice how similar her room is to mine. There are just a few subtle differences, but for the most part, they're the same.

"I'd offer you a drink, but you already have two," she says with a laugh. "Have a seat." She points toward the small table and chairs, and we sit down.

"I haven't played truth or dare in years," I say. "How do we play again?"

"I haven't played in years either, but I think the rules are easy. I'll start... ready?"

I nod. "Ready as ever."

"Truth or dare," she says.

"Truth," I say with a grin. I can't just jump in headfirst with a dare... you have to work up to that.

She puts her finger to her chin as though she's thinking of a question to ask me. "How about... Did you ever have a crush on me when we were younger?"

Well, she's getting right to the good stuff.

"Well..." I squirm in my seat, surprised that she asked me this right off the bat. Sure, I was hoping this game would give me a chance to get closer to her, but I thought she'd start with some warm-up questions first. If she can be this direct, so can I. "Yes. I did."

Her lips curl up. "You did?"

I nod and lean closer to her. "Yeah, I did. I thought you were cute. And nice. Whenever our families got together, I felt a little nervous around you."

Monique bites her lip, speechless, then sips her Coke.

I lean back in my chair and continue. "Truth or dare?"

Monique sets her drink down on the table and looks at me. "Truth."

I might as well ask her the same thing. I'm curious what she thought of me when we were younger. "Did you have a crush on me?"

She squirms in her seat. "*Did* I have a crush on you?"

I wait for her to answer, but then I realize she emphasized the word *did*. "Or *do* you have a crush on me?" I ask, being even more bold.

Her eyes meet mine. *Please say yes...*

She slowly nods her head. "Yes. I do have a crush on you, Kevin."

My heart pounds in my chest. "Is that right?"

She nods again. "Yeah, I do. Truth or dare?" she asks, quickly continuing our game.

"Truth," I say automatically.

"Do you have a crush on me?"

"Yes. Truth or dare?" I ask, picking up the pace of our questions.

"Dare," she says, sitting closer to the edge of her seat.

Thank God. "I dare you to kiss me."

Time seems to stand still. Monique looks into my eyes, then asks, "You want me to kiss you?"

"Very much so," I reply, hoping she'll accept her dare.

Monique stands, so I stand, too. She steps closer to me, still looking into my eyes, and wraps her hand around my head, pulling my lips down to hers. As soon as we make contact, a spark ignites inside me. I wrap my arms around her waist and pull her closer.

My heart races as my teenage dream comes true. Monique's lips move with mine, our tongues glide together, and it feels good—*really* good—to kiss and hold her like this.

Suddenly, she pulls her lips back but doesn't step away. She looks at me, her hand still holding the base of my neck, her other hand resting on my hip. "Truth or dare?" Her voice is hoarse, practically a whisper, and her expression makes me believe she wants more.

"Dare," I say, curious about what she'll say next.

"I dare you to touch me."

Fuck. That's all I need to hear. I don't hesitate and crash my lips to hers again, moving us closer to her bed. If this is what she wants, I'll give it to her. We've spent the past couple of days getting to know each other again after all these years, and I like her—a lot. I'm going to touch Monique everywhere she wants to be touched, and I'll make her feel better than any other man has before.

This is my dream come true.

6

MONIQUE

"Close the curtains." My voice comes out shaky as Kevin kisses my neck, sending goose bumps all over my body. My plan worked, and I have Kevin right where I want him—in my bed.

But before we can get down and dirty, we need to close the curtains in front of the sliding glass door. The last thing I want is someone to walk by and see us... especially if that someone is one of our family members.

"Okay. Hang on," he says, getting off the bed and granting my request. It doesn't take him very long, and he crawls onto the bed again.

"You're beautiful," he says, brushing my hair back, making my body quiver with anticipation.

"You're sexy," I say, and then we're all lips and tongues again, kissing each other senseless.

A rush of excitement surges through me. I can't believe Kevin Blake is kissing me, touching my body. And I can't believe I like it. In fact, I can't get enough of it. His hand cups my breast, but the feeling over my clothing isn't enough. I need to feel him skin to skin.

I tug his shirt up and caress his back. He moans, letting me know he likes my touch. He reaches up and pulls his shirt over his head, tossing it to the floor before reaching for the hem of my shirt. I sit up, and he drags it up and over my head. I'm wearing my bikini underneath, so his fingers deftly untie it behind my back. The loose fabric pulls away from my breasts, then falls, my nipples hardening at the sudden exposure. I throw my bikini top to the floor to join both our shirts, and when I look back at Kevin, I see the heat in his eyes.

"You're so sexy," he says, leaning closer, teasing me with his lips. "I want you."

He kisses my neck, and my whole body responds. "I want you, too," I whisper, hoping he'll touch me where I need it most.

His lips kiss down my neck to my breasts. I lie back against the pillows as he covers one nipple with his mouth and the other with his hand. It's pure heaven as Kevin worships my body, making me feel more incredible than anyone's ever made me feel before. Every nerve ending is on fire, burning with desire for more of him.

My eyes close as I enjoy what he's doing to me. Wetness pools at my core, and I move my hips, hoping he'll take the hint.

He does.

His hand drops to the apex of my thighs, and his

fingers begin exploring. I spread my legs to give him access, and he takes full advantage, lightly caressing the most sensitive part of my body before slipping his finger inside. His mouth continues to suck and lick my puckered nipple while he pushes deeper inside me. He crooks his finger at just the right angle and hits that special spot that not all men know how to find.

Kevin knows what he's doing.

My entire body clenches as I come undone, screaming a garbled mix of words.

Holy fuck. That was incredible. I think I've won the jackpot because Kevin knows exactly what to do to make me come.

He quickly gets up to get a condom, giving me a moment to collect myself. He rolls it onto his impressive length before returning to where we left off. He kisses me sweetly as he pushes inside, and my eyes close once again. He's a little bigger than I've had in the past, but my body stretches to accommodate his size.

Kevin stills. "Are you okay?"

I nod. "Yeah. Better than okay."

He doesn't say anything. He just presses his lips to mine again as he starts moving at a steady pace. His dick slides in deep, pushing me closer to another orgasm. He seems to worship my body as we move together.

And then it happens—he sends me over the edge again, and I moan in pleasure as my body trembles beneath him. With just a few more thrusts, Kevin stills, grunting loudly as he climaxes inside me.

As we lie together, naked, trying to calm our breathing, it hits me that this really happened. I had sex with Kevin Blake. Never in a million years would my teenage self believe me if I said that shy, nerdy Kevin would turn out to be a hot, sexy man who knows how to pleasure a woman. But it's true. I slept with Kevin, and it was fantastic. He made me come faster and harder than any man has before.

Happy Thanksgiving to me!

As I walk into The Bistro, I feel as if I'm floating. I've just had the best sex of my life and can't wait to see Kevin again. But I'm also nervous. Will it be obvious to everyone else that something's going on between Kevin and me? We have to act naturally so no one catches onto our fling. Neither Kevin nor I want anyone in our families to find out we slept together. That could make things complicated real fast. Before he left my room, we agreed to keep things a secret.

I make eye contact with Mom, and she waves me over. It looks like I'm not the last to arrive. Kevin, Kyle, and Sarah still aren't here. My mind flashes back to how good it felt when Kevin first slid inside me. I can still feel how full he felt between my legs as I walk toward the table.

"Hi, Monique!" Mom, Dad, Kathy, Dan, Adeline, and Andre all greet me, and I have to stop replaying the scene of Kevin fucking me in my head.

"Hi!" Was my voice shaky? Do I appear nervous?

I sit in one of the four empty seats, three of which are all right next to each other on one side of the table. Kathy is directly across from me, Adeline is to my right, and Mom is across from her.

"Hey, sis," she says. "What'd you do all day?"

I take a sip of the water that's already been poured for me. I have to be truthful about Kevin and me hanging out since Kyle and Sarah saw us together even though they're not here yet. I'm guessing Kyle is still passed out. I wonder if Sarah will join us for dinner? Regardless, they know Kevin and I were together, so I can't lie about spending the day with him.

I just can't mention how he returned to my room and gave me multiple orgasms.

I set my glass of water down. "Well, first I slept in, which felt great. I think I've finally adjusted to the time difference here. Then Kevin and I both happened to be drinking coffee out on our front porches, and we were bored, so we decided to borrow one of the hotel's kayaks and paddle out in the water for a bit."

"Oh, fun!" Mom doesn't seem weirded out by the fact that Kevin and I hung out together, so that's good.

"Did you see any cool fish out there?" Dad asks, who also seems unfazed.

"We saw some jellyfish and a few jumping fish," I reply. "But nothing like the fish we saw at Silk Caye."

Mom and Dad's eyes look up at something behind me, and the hairs on the back of my neck stand on end. Kevin's here.

"Hey, everyone," he says, and I turn to look at him.

He sits in the chair beside me and smiles as we make eye contact. God, he's sexy. My entire body suddenly feels a magnetic force pulsing between us, and I wonder if he feels it, too. I want to reach out and touch him, but I can't. This is going to be torture.

"Monique was just telling us how the two of you went kayaking today," his mom says.

"Oh yeah, that was fun," he says casually. He looks at me briefly before turning back to his mom. "We also went to the bowling alley down the street."

"You did?" his dad, sitting across from him, says. "I was wondering about that place. It looks so small. How many bowling lanes do they have?"

"Only four," Kevin replies with a chuckle. "It's the smallest bowling alley I've ever been to, but it was a great little place. We had a good time."

Kevin turns to look at me again, and his hand hovers above mine for a split second before he reaches for his water glass. Was that my imagination, or was he about to put his hand on mine before suddenly remembering he can't do that in front of our families? Is he feeling the same way I am, wanting to touch me right now? That magnetic pulse between us still hasn't died down either.

"Are Kyle and Sarah going to join us?" Kevin asks his parents. I'm sure he knows the answer to that question, but, like me, he's probably curious to hear what his parents have to say.

They both shrug before his mom answers, "We don't know. Sarah returned the keys to the SUV and said Kyle wasn't feeling well. We told her she could still join us for

Thanksgiving dinner even if he doesn't, but I don't know if she will."

Kevin and I both nod, and then Dad changes the subject. "So who won at bowling?"

I turn to look at him and smile widely. "I did, of course!"

Everyone laughs at my cockiness. "That's my girl," Dad says. "You were always good at bowling."

"Good job," Mom adds.

"Yeah, I had no idea how good she was." Kevin glances at me, giving me a knowing look that makes me think he's not just talking about bowling.

My belly muscles clench as I remember how good he was with his hands... his mouth... his cock...

All thoughts are interrupted when our server arrives to take our order.

We make it through dinner—minus Kyle and Sarah—without anyone being the wiser about Kevin and me sleeping together. That pulsing feeling hasn't waned, though. I'm dying to touch him again, and I can only hope I'll get that chance at least once more before we leave Belize.

After our unconventional Thanksgiving dinner, everyone decides to walk out on the beach again. It's a beautiful evening with the moon and stars shining bright overhead. We all walk out onto the thatch roof dock. It's a little unnerving without any railings around it, especially in the dark. We're able to see where we're going, though, due to the light under the covered area. The only sound we hear, besides our own footsteps, is the gentle waves lapping against the wood pilings below us.

I wish I could wrap my arms around Kevin right now. What a romantic spot to be, and our family members are taking full advantage. Mom and Dad sit on the bench swing, and Andre and Adeline crawl onto the hammock together. Dan and Kathy stand hand in hand with her head on his shoulder, looking back toward the hotel, enjoying the peacefulness out here.

Kevin and I stand next to one another but not close enough. He looks at me, and I look at him, but we don't say anything. I don't think there's anything either of us can say right now that we'd want anyone else to hear. All I can think about is being in bed with him again, his hands roaming my body.

Dan and Kathy turn around. He asks my dad, "What time do you think we should leave for the waterfall tomorrow?"

"After breakfast," Dad replies. "Around ten or eleven."

"Should we all meet for breakfast and then leave?" Kathy suggests.

"Sure," Mom replies before turning to face Kevin and me. "Does that sound good?"

I nod. "Yeah. I'll be there."

"Me, too," Kevin says.

Tomorrow, everyone will head out on another excursion together. We're going to see a beautiful waterfall not far from here, which I'm looking forward to seeing. The thought of spending all day with Kevin again excites me...

but we'll also be surrounded by our families, which means we'll have to behave.

After spending a little time out on the dock, we all decide to walk back to shore. Kathy expresses her concern about Kyle and Sarah, so Kevin agrees to go check on them. Unfortunately, that means I end up going back to my hut all alone. That's okay, though. Tomorrow is a new day, and I'll get to spend it with my new crush.

7

MONIQUE

"Well, well, well. He's alive," Dan jokes as Kyle and Sarah join us at our table in The Bistro.

Kyle rolls his eyes, then sits down. "I got food poisoning or something."

Or you were drunk.

"I'm glad you're feeling better," Kathy says.

Everyone is here for breakfast now, except Kevin. I turn to see if he's walking in yet, but I don't see him.

"Today should be a fun outing," Dad says. "According to some articles I read, the Maya King Waterfalls are some of the most picturesque in Belize."

"I can't wait," Mom says.

"Do we have to hike far to see them?" Kathy asks.

"No, it's supposed to be a short walk from the parking lot," Dad explains.

"Are you going to jump in for a swim?" Dan asks Kyle, who looks at his dad like he's crazy.

He's such an ass.

"That depends," Kyle says. "If it's not too cold and swimmable, then hell yeah, I'll jump in."

"People do swim there," Dad tells him, and I wonder why both Dan and my dad are encouraging Kyle. I can only imagine he'll be obnoxious about it now.

Kyle links his fingers together, stretches his arms in front of him, and cracks his knuckles. "Well, I guess I'll have to give it a try, then," he says smugly.

"You'll have to give what a try?" Kevin's voice surprises me from behind.

I turn to see him, and he looks right at me. We smile at one another before he sits in the last empty chair available, which is unfortunately a couple down from me.

Everyone tells him good morning, and then Kyle explains what he was talking about before our server arrives to take our drink orders. I order coffee. I about fall over in my chair when Kyle orders a Bloody Mary. *Great.* He's starting the day off drinking. Hopefully, he'll behave himself today, especially since he'll be around his parents.

Since Kevin and I are sitting a couple of seats apart on the same side of the table, it's not easy for me to see him. We do make eye contact a few times throughout breakfast, and each time we do, I feel a jolt of electricity. He looks so damn attractive in the blue shirt he's wearing. It makes his blue eyes stand out more. He looks like sex on a stick, and I'm craving more with him.

After we finish breakfast, everyone heads toward the parking lot together. I'm glad when Kevin casually chooses to walk beside me. "Hey," he says. "How are you today?"

"I'm good. How about you? Did you sleep well?"

"Yeah," he replies before leaning closer to me and saying quietly, "I missed you, though."

Oh. My heart pounds a little harder in my chest. It's exhilarating to know he missed me since I missed him, too.

We're walking behind everyone else, and none of them pay any attention to us. "I missed you, too," I say quietly.

He smiles, then gently rubs my arm. We reach the two rental cars parked next to each other. His family is getting into theirs, and my family is getting into ours. "I'll see you there," he says, subtly touching my hand and squeezing it before walking around to his parents' SUV.

I wish we could ride together, sitting close in the back seat, touching each other every chance we get... but that's not possible.

I get into my parents' SUV, and Dad starts the engine.

The drive to the waterfalls is only about thirty minutes. I wasn't sure what to expect when we got there, but it wasn't what I thought it would be like at all. First of all, when we pulled off the highway onto the road leading to the falls, there's a large replica of a Mayan temple near the ticket booth. The waterfalls are inside a park you must pay to get into. The road leading to the waterfalls is a long dirt road. There are horses behind a fence at first, and then lots of trees. Some of them look like orange trees, and I'm intrigued. We're heading into what looks like a jungle ahead, and I have to admit I've never seen anywhere like this before.

We finally come to a second gate, where a man waits to take a ticket given to us at the ticket booth. The man manually opens the gate for us, and we drive through. The road starts going uphill, and before long, we're in a parking lot. Dad pulls into an empty space and cuts the engine. "We're here," he says, and it reminds me of when we'd go on outings as kids. Dad always ended the car ride with, "We're here."

We all pile out of the car, as do the Blakes who parked next to us. Kevin and I immediately make eye contact and smile at one another. Adeline and Andre hold hands, and I wish Kevin and I could do that. I would love to feel his hand in mine as we walk through this beautiful jungle.

That's not going to happen, though.

"This looks like the path we take," Dad says, leading the way.

Everyone follows him. I hang back, hoping Kevin does the same so we can walk together, and he does. "It's beautiful here," he says as we walk side by side.

"Yeah, it is. I didn't realize we'd be in the jungle."

"Neither did I. Although, now that I think about it, from the plane we flew into Placencia on, the land below looked like a jungle, so I guess this makes sense."

"I remember that, too," I reply, thinking back to my flight on the tiny plane. "I can't believe how small that plane was. Have you ever been on such a small airplane before?"

He chuckles. "No. And I was pretty apprehensive about getting on that one. I'm not looking forward to flying back to Belize City when it's time to go home."

"Neither am I," I agree, although having to get onto such a small aircraft again isn't the only reason I'm not looking forward to flying back. Leaving Belize also means saying goodbye to Kevin, and I don't want to think about that right now.

Everyone ahead of us stops walking, so we stop, too. "What is it?" I ask. There's not a waterfall in sight.

"It's just a pretty view of the creek," Dad says. "I wanted to stop for a picture."

He's right; the view is beautiful. I look up at the canopy. We are in a jungle, and I've never been anywhere like this. The sunlight peeks through the palm fronds and other leaves above us, and the creek below sparkles as it flows.

"This is amazing," I say quietly.

"Yeah, it is," Kevin agrees.

Everyone starts walking again, so we follow. It doesn't take long for us to come to a clearing, and we see a building. However, the building isn't enclosed, it's open.

"What is this place?" Adeline says aloud.

"It's a bar!" Of course, Kyle recognizes a bar when he sees one.

It's not open for a business, though. It looks like an open area to have a party. There are tables and chairs about, as well as the bar, but they're empty.

"You must be able to rent this place for events," Mom says, speculating on why this place is here.

"What a cool spot," Kathy says as we walk through. We can hear the waterfall as we get to the other side of the covered bar area.

"There it is!" Dad points ahead, and as I get closer, I see the cascading water falling over a cliff into a pool of water.

"Wow," I say, slipping my phone out of my pocket to take pictures.

We all continue moving on the path, closer to the waterfall. The trail takes us uphill, and soon we realize it's leading to the second waterfall, which is even more breathtaking than the first. Everyone oohs and aahs at the amazing sight and takes pictures.

Another couple walks by, and Dad asks them to take a photo of our whole group. They oblige, so we all gather with the waterfall in the background. Of course, Kevin and I stand next to each other. To my surprise, he puts his arm around me.

I whip my head to look at him, but he smirks at me, then turns his head to look at the camera. I turn forward as well, smiling for the picture. All the while, my mind races: how will Kevin and I look in the picture, standing next to one another with his arm around me? Will anyone comment on how we're standing together? Does he feel the same pull of attraction toward me that I feel toward him? Will we hook up again while we're still in Belize?

What will happen between us when it's time to go home?

That last question has been in the back of my mind all day, and I don't want to think about it. I want to shove that thought aside and forget it even exists. Right now, I only want to enjoy my vacation and enjoy Kevin's company as much as possible... without anyone in our families finding out.

After taking the picture, Dad looks at his phone. "The picture turned out great," he says, not mentioning anything about the way Kevin and I stood together. I guess we didn't look suspicious after all.

We all continue wandering around the area, enjoying the view. Then suddenly, Sarah squeals. "Are you serious?"

I turn my head and see that Kyle has taken his shirt off. "Yeah, I am. I'm going to jump in!"

Oh lord.

Sarah shakes her head in exasperation. "I can't believe you. That water is cold!"

Kyle scoffs. "I'll be fine!"

Famous last words.

"Kyle, be careful," Kathy says. "Is it even legal for you to jump in? I don't want a park ranger to arrest you."

Kyle laughs at his mom. "No one's going to arrest me, Mom."

"It's okay for him to jump in," Dad explains. "I read that people swim here all the time... usually in the summer months when it's warmer, though."

"I'll be fine," Kyle says again, kicking his shoes off. "It'll be like a polar plunge. I'll feel invigorated afterward."

"I can't watch," Sarah says, turning around and walking away.

"Kevin, get this on video," Kyle instructs his brother as he rubs his hands together, warming up for his jump.

Kevin rolls his eyes but gets his phone ready anyway. "Okay, go for it," he tells Kyle, recording on his phone.

Kyle steps closer to the edge, looking into the water below. It's not a far jump into the pool of water, but I bet it's colder than he's anticipating.

"All right, here goes nothing!" Kyle claps his hands

together, then jumps off the rock he's standing on into the water below. He disappears underwater with a loud splash before reemerging a moment later. As he takes a breath of air, he shouts a loud, "Woo!" and his mouth forms an O shape. "It's cold! Get my towel out of my backpack," he demands to no one in particular as he moves quickly to where he can pull himself up and out of the water.

I look at Sarah, who turns around to see him. She shakes her head and mutters, "Idiot," then heads toward his backpack to retrieve his towel for him.

I shake my head, too, but for different reasons. Kyle and Sarah are both interesting people with an interesting relationship. I can't believe they're engaged to be married. Neither of them seems mature enough to be joined in holy matrimony yet. I don't see what Sarah sees in Kyle since she always seems annoyed with whatever he's doing. Not that I blame her. I'm annoyed with Kyle, too... but I'm not engaged to the guy.

As he gets out of the water, Kevin walks over and gently touches my arm. "Hey," he says, "follow me."

"What?" I turn to look at him, but he's already walking away, following the path away from our group.

Where is he going? Will our families notice we're both missing?

Everyone seems occupied with Kyle's antics right now, so I say *screw it* and follow Kevin up the path, then around a corner, out of view of everyone else.

As soon as I turn the corner, Kevin wraps his arms around me, pulling my body flush to his, and his mouth covers mine in a searing, hot kiss. I moan, melting into this man and his strong arms. Holding him tight, I don't want to let go. I don't want this kiss to end.

But then it does.

"Sorry," Kevin says, resting his forehead against mine. "I couldn't wait another minute to kiss you."

My heart skips a beat. It's good to know he wants me just as much as I want him.

"Don't apologize," I say, wrapping my arms around his neck. "Just kiss me again."

Our lips connect once more, our tongues moving together, each of us giving and taking just the right amount. His fingers tangle in my hair, pulling ever so slightly, and I gently bite his bottom lip.

He moans into my mouth. My entire body responds to him, and I want more. I *need* more of Kevin, and it'll be hard waiting to be alone with him again. Hopefully, we'll have the opportunity later at the hotel... maybe he can come to my hut again...

He pulls away much too soon. "This is risky," he says, his voice barely above a whisper for fear of someone hearing us. "We should get back to our families."

I nod but then pull his lips to mine again. Just one more quick kiss...

Footsteps on the dirt path behind me alert me to stop, so I quickly pull back from him. Instantly, I miss his touch.

And then two people we don't know walk past us.

It wasn't anyone in our families walking on the path. We could've continued that blissful kiss.

We look at each other and laugh.

"Come on. We should join our families before they

wonder where we ran off to," he says, gently taking my arm and leading me down the path we took to get to this secluded spot.

Unfortunately, he doesn't keep his hand on me as we continue walking.

It doesn't take long for us to find everyone, who has now moved back toward the first waterfall. No one even noticed we were gone.

"What's that up there?" Mom asks, pointing at a stone-covered building.

"I don't know. Let's check it out," Dad says, so we all follow him up another trail to the unusual building.

There's a fancy wood-carved door on the front of the building. Nothing explains this building, so Dad takes it upon himself to open the door. To his and everyone else's surprise, it's unlocked. "Whoa, this is cool," Dad says as he walks in.

The rest of us follow, and as soon as I see the inside, I'm shocked. It's an unfinished hotel room of sorts. There's a bed frame, built-in dresser, and an attached bathroom only halfway done.

"It looks like they never finished the construction," Dan says as he looks around the peculiar room.

"How bizarre," Kathy says. "But this would be an amazing place to spend the night. Right next to the water-falls and all."

Mom's eyes light up. "Maybe the owners intended for this place to be an all-inclusive spot for parties—or weddings! People could have their reception down in the covered bar area, then the bride and groom can spend the night in the bridal suite here."

"We should buy this place and open it just for that," Kathy says to Mom. "We could make a fortune."

Mom nods her head. "I'm in," she says with a laugh.

"I'd get married here," Sarah says. "This would be so romantic."

Kyle rolls his eyes at his fiancée. "Nah. We should just go to Vegas."

Sarah crosses her arms over her chest. "Vegas? No. We are *not* having some tacky ceremony at a casino."

Kyle laughs. "Babe, you can have nice weddings in Vegas! They offer all kinds."

She rolls her eyes. "Whatever. I'm saying no to Vegas. I want our wedding to be classy."

"Vegas is classy," Kyle says, rolling his eyes again. "You just don't know."

Sarah shakes her head, then turns and starts walking toward the door. "I *do* know, and I *don't* want to get married in Vegas," she says as she practically stomps out of the room.

Everything between Sarah and Kyle seems to escalate quickly.

Kyle follows her out the door, presumably to apologize.

"Well, then," Mom says, trying to shift the energy in the room. "Shall we head back down now?"

"Sure," Dad agrees, then leads the way.

Once again, Kevin and I are the last to leave, and he takes my hand to stop me from leaving the unfinished hotel room. I look at him, surprised.

"Just one more kiss," he says as he puts his hands on either side of my face and pulls me closer.

Kissing Kevin feels good. *Too* good. I wish we could do more than just kiss right now.

When we finally return to the Maya Beach Hotel, everyone agrees to do our own thing until dinner. Kevin walks beside me as we follow our family members toward our rooms. They continue walking past our huts to their building, so we say goodbye. As soon as they're out of sight, Kevin turns to me and asks, "Can I come in?"

Of course, I agree, and it takes less than a minute for us to end up half naked on my bed.

"You're so fucking sexy," Kevin says, crashing his mouth down on mine.

The passion between us is so strong, I feel it throughout my body. It's like electricity flowing through my veins, and his touch rocks me to my core. I don't think I've ever felt anything like this before.

His hand finds my breast, pulling and rolling the nipple between his fingers. I moan as my body surrenders to the pleasure. His tongue explores my skin before settling on my other nipple. He licks around the tip before sucking it in his mouth. I fist his hair, feeling myself getting closer to release.

His hand skims down my body and gently pushes my legs apart. I gasp when his finger circles my clit, sending electric tingles to every nerve ending in my body. I move my hips against him, needing more in order to release the pressure building inside...

And then I do. "Fuck! Kevin!" I call out his name as my body erupts. Kevin

continues everything he's doing, sending me over the edge. My orgasm doesn't stop as wave after wave moves through me.

I've never felt so much pleasure all at once. Sex with Kevin is definitely an experience that I won't soon forget. I try to catch my breath and wipe the beads of sweat from my forehead. Kevin retrieves a condom and slides it onto his cock, then he's over me again. He kisses my cheek, then my nose, then I feel the head of his cock at my entrance.

"I've thought about this all day," he says as he begins to push in. "I want you, Monique. You're so fucking amazing."

As he slides in deep, he links his fingers with mine. This time feels more intimate than before, and I wonder what that could mean.

But I don't want to think right now. I just want to enjoy my time with Kevin. I want to feel his touch and revel in everything he does to bring me pleasure.

So that's exactly what I do.

I close my eyes as Kevin fucks me. He kisses my lips, and our tongues slide together sensually as his cock continues to hit that special spot deep inside. One of his hands lets go of mine to fondle my breast, tugging lightly on my nipple. It's all so much, and I know I'll plummet over the edge at any moment.

"Yes. Just like that. Don't stop." My voice is breathy as I tell him what I need, and before I know it, I'm coming again.

"You're so sexy when you come," he says softly as my

body trembles in pleasure. "Your pussy feels so good. I won't last long."

Kevin slows his movements, fucking me at a gentle pace. He feels incredible, and I feel as if I'm on fire. Every nerve ending stings, and I know I'm on the brink of another orgasm. No one has ever made me come so hard before.

Kevin increases his pace as he nibbles my neck, making his way down to my breast. His skilled tongue swirls my nipple, and my body sings with pleasure. As he sucks it in his mouth, I come apart again.

Despite saying he wouldn't last long, Kevin lasts a long time. Every time he feels close to coming, he tapers back, then focuses on pleasuring me with his mouth and hands until he can fuck me again. By the time he does release, I come with him. I've never had so many orgasms at one time. My body feels like jelly, and I'm in awe of Kevin. The way he touches my body, it's as if he's worshiping me. My feelings for him are growing, and I find that a little terrifying.

I can't allow myself to think like that, though. I just want to enjoy my time with Kevin while I'm here. It's premature to be worrying about feelings anyway. I'll be back home in Paris next week, and he'll be in Seattle. There's no time to develop feelings. What happens in Belize stays in Belize... right?

8

KEVIN

My eyes flutter open, but I promptly shut them again. I'm tired and don't want to wake up yet. This bed is comfy, and hearing the waves hit the shore outside is relaxing. Last night with Monique was amazing. The first time we slept together a couple of nights ago was good, but last night... just wow. Who knew Monique and I would have such incredible chemistry?

Wait...

I open my eyes again and see a different picture hanging on the wall. I roll over and find Monique asleep beside me. I'm in her room, not mine. I fell asleep here.

This wouldn't be an issue if we weren't trying to keep our fling a secret from our families. However, the light through the crack in the curtains tells me the sun is coming up, and I don't want anyone to see me leaving Monique's hut.

I rub my eyes, then get out of bed. I grab my phone on the nightstand and see it's barely six o'clock. I'm sure no one in our families will be up yet. I haven't woken up this early since being in Belize, and I wonder if I'll be greeted with an unbelievable sunrise when I leave Monique's room.

After dinner last night, I came back to Monique's room with her. It seems impossible for us to keep our hands off each other, and I craved her again. The sex is so good between us, it's unbelievable. I want to savor it while we're here in Belize because I know our time together has an expiration date. Before we know it, we'll be returning to our own lives, thousands of miles apart.

Monique stirs as I get dressed. Just as I pull my shirt over my head, she wakes up. "What time is it?" she asks, her voice sounding dazed.

"Just after six," I reply, looking for my flip-flops. "I fell asleep with you."

"Oh," she says, yawning. She sits up and looks at me. "It should be fine. I'm sure no one else is up yet."

I find my flip-flops, which got kicked under the bed, and slide them onto my feet. "Yeah, I'm sure I'm in the clear."

Although it's fairly dark in the room, I can still see Monique's beautiful face. I walk around to her side of the bed, and her eyes look up to meet mine. I don't want to leave without kissing her goodbye even though I'll see her again in a few short hours. I wish I didn't have to leave now.

I lean down and kiss her. "I'll see you soon."

"Okay," she says and yawns again.

I kiss her forehead, then turn to leave. As soon as I

move the curtain back to open the sliding glass door, I observe the most gorgeous sunrise I've ever seen. She has to see this. "Monique, look at this," I say, holding the curtain open for her to view.

She slowly sits up to look, and as soon as her eyes adjust to the beautiful sight, she gasps. "Oh my gosh." She gets out of bed and walks over to join me at the door. "I want to go out and see it."

I slide the door open, and we both walk outside. The beach is empty, so we're not worried about anyone seeing us. The breathtaking view has hues of orange and yellow on the horizon over the water. We can't *not* enjoy it.

Wearing only a T-shirt and a pair of sexy pink underwear, neither of which barely covers her ass, Monique is absolutely stunning, leaning against the porch railing. My fingers itch to touch her... I'd love nothing more than to take her back into her room and have my way with her. I want to take full advantage of my time with Monique. Since we have to sneak around our families, our alone time is limited.

I walk to the railing and stand beside her, our shoulders touching. "It was worth getting out of bed to see this," she says, looking at the beautiful splendor before us.

Suddenly, a couple of people walking along the shore come into view. It's Adeline and Andre. My first instinct is to get out of sight so they don't see Monique and me together on her porch this early in the morning. However, they stop walking and stand with their backs to us, watching the sunrise with their arms around each other, and for some reason, I stay where I am.

"Um, should we go inside?" Monique whispers, although they're far enough away from us that she probably could've said it in her normal voice.

And then it happens. Andre gets down on one knee in front of Adeline.

"Oh my gosh!" Monique's hands fly to her face, and she's clearly excited for her sister.

We watch Adeline nod, and Andre slips a ring onto her finger. He stands, wraps her in a hug, and they kiss. As exciting as this is, I still feel as if I need to get off Monique's porch before they see us.

But then it's too late.

Adeline turns her head and sees us. She stops, as if she's trying to figure out if she sees what she thinks she sees. Andre turns to see what she's looking at, and now they're both looking at us.

Shit.

"Oh crap," Monique says, pushing away from the railing. "What do we do?"

I rub the back of my neck as Adeline and Andre start walking toward us. Monique doesn't have any pants on. "Go put on some pants," I suggest. "I'll just make something up."

She tugs on her T-shirt so it covers her more. "Okay," she says, then quickly turns and goes inside her hut.

Adeline and Andre walk up to the porch, standing on the beach in front of me. "Hey, Kevin," Adeline says, her eyebrows knitted in as if she's confused to see me here on her sister's porch... which makes sense. "Whatcha doin'?"

I need a believable excuse, so I go with the only logical

one I can think of. "I woke up early to watch the sunrise, and when I came outside, Monique was out on her porch watching it, too. So I came over here to enjoy it with her."

Adeline eyes me skeptically while Andre tries to wipe the knowing smile from his face. *Fuck.* "Why did my sister disappear when we started walking toward you guys?"

"Oh. She had to, um—"

"Put shorts on," Monique finishes my sentence as she walks out onto the porch with her pajama shorts now on. "I was so excited to see the sunrise, I came out here in just my T-shirt. Then I realized I wasn't wearing pants, and— wait! Are congratulations in order, little sis? Did we see what we think we saw happen over there?"

Nice deflection...

Adeline's face breaks out in a smile. She holds her left hand out for us to see, which now has a huge sparkling diamond on the ring finger. "Yes! Andre proposed, and I said yes!"

"Oh my gosh!" Monique runs down the porch stairs to her sister and gives her a hug.

I follow and shake Andre's hand. "Congrats, man."

"Thanks." He gives me a knowing grin, leans in closer, and whispers, "And congrats to you, too?" He winks, and I know he's referring to Monique and me being together.

Before I can respond, Monique steals Andre for a hug, so I congratulate Adeline with a hug as well.

"What a romantic way to propose," Monique says to Andre. "How'd you convince her to wake up so early?"

"I can be convincing sometimes," he says with a chuckle as he puts his arm around Adeline. "I just told her

I wanted us to see the sunrise at least once in Belize. Last night, she agreed to wake up early for it, so today was the day."

Adeline turns toward Andre with her mouth hanging open. "You mean if I had agreed to wake up early yesterday, you would've proposed to me then?"

"Yep," he says. "I wanted to do it at sunrise to be memorable."

"What if I decided to *never* wake up early to see the sunrise?" she asks.

He shrugs. "Then I guess we'd never get engaged." He cracks a smile to let her know he's joking, and she playfully hits his arm.

Monique beams at her little sister and future brother-in-law. "This is so exciting! And I can't believe we got to witness it! When are you going to tell Mom and Dad?"

"At breakfast, I guess," Adeline replies.

"Do Mom and Dad know you were going to propose?" Monique asks Andre.

He nods. "Yeah, I already talked to them about it, and they gave me their blessing."

Adeline's mouth drops open in surprise again. "You did? Oh, baby, that's so sweet."

"Aw, I bet Mom cried," Monique says.

Andre nods. "She did. Your dad even got a little teary."

"I can't wait to tell them," Adeline says.

I suddenly feel like an outsider. As if I'm intruding on a special Blanchet family moment. "Well, congrats, guys. I'm gonna head back to my room for a shower."

"Thanks, Kevin," Adeline says.

Andre says bye, and so does Monique, who smiles sweetly at me before I walk away. Last night with Monique was incredible. Watching the sunrise with her this morning was amazing. But now... after watching Adeline and Andre's romantic moment on the beach, I feel the need to define what's going on between Monique and me. We only have two days left together here in Belize before she goes back to Paris and I go back home to Seattle. Are we going to stay in touch? Or just say goodbye and maybe see each other again in another decade?

The truth is, I'd like to find the love of my life. Seeing how happy Adeline and Andre are together solidified the fact that I'd like to have a woman to share my life with. My parents have been married for over thirty years, and I want a love like they have. I want to have a family someday. Even my brother is engaged to the woman he loves. Sure, I'm only twenty-eight years old, and I have plenty of time to find a wife. But one thing I've realized over these past few days is that Monique is everything I've ever wanted in a partner.

These are scary thoughts to be having. I've known Monique my entire life. Our parents are best friends. We're just having a good time together while we're in Belize.

But the thought of not seeing her again scares the crap out of me.

I *want* to see her again. And I don't want to wait another ten years to do it. I want Monique to be in my life, and I want to be in hers. Things would be so much easier if we lived on the same continent, though.

As I get in the shower, I want to wash all these thoughts

away. I realize I'm being ridiculous. Monique and I went into this fling with an understanding. We're just having fun. For Christ's sake—we're both young, and I'm totally jumping the gun with all these thoughts. I need to get my head out of my ass and simply enjoy my time with her while it lasts. I don't need to worry about the future right now.

***

"Congratulations!" Everyone congratulates Adeline and Andre at breakfast. Love is in the air, and Kyle is even being sweet and lovey toward Sarah this morning. Maybe he's kissing her ass after being a dipshit, but whatever the reason, I suddenly feel lonely surrounded by my family and friends.

Monique looks at me from her seat across the table. She smiles, though there's a hint of sadness in it. I wonder what she's thinking. Is she feeling alone like me? We're the only two singles here with our families, yet we've had a fantastic time together on this trip. Albeit, nobody knows just how good of a time we've had together here.

Maybe it has to do with the fact that her younger sister just got engaged. If *I'm* having all these thoughts about being single, perhaps she is, too. It's *her* sister who got engaged, after all. Regardless of what the reason might be, all I want to do is make her feel better.

After breakfast, all the women decide to go shopping in town, and Dad and Mr. Blanchet decide to go golfing. They invite Andre, Kyle, and me to join them, but the three of us decline. Golf has never been my thing, and I'd rather spend the day here at the hotel.

Everyone gets up to leave, except Andre, Kyle, and me. "You boys wanna hang out and get a drink?" Kyle asks.

To my surprise, Andre agrees. "It's five o'clock somewhere, right?"

Since I don't have anything else to do, and I don't want to be antisocial with Andre and my brother, I agree. "Sure, why not?"

We get up and move to the bar. We're the only ones sitting here, but considering it's not even eleven o'clock yet, that's not entirely surprising.

"What can I get you?" the Belizean bartender asks.

"I'll have a Bloody Mary," Kyle says. This'll be his second today. I want to keep tabs on how much he drinks so he doesn't make an ass of himself later.

"I'll have the same," Andre replies.

The bartender turns to me. "I'll have a Belikin." I've become fond of the Belizean beer. I wonder if I can find it anywhere in the States. It's advertised everywhere we go here, but I'd never heard of it before.

"Congrats again, man," Kyle says to Andre. "Adeline's a great girl."

"Thanks. I appreciate that," Andre says. "How long have you and Sarah been engaged?"

"A few months," Kyle replies. "I proposed at the beach, too. We were on the Santa Monica Pier."

"That's cool. Are you going to get married in Southern California?"

"We don't know yet, but probably somewhere close to

where we live. I don't really care where it is. She can plan it all, and I'll show up for the party." Kyle laughs.

Andre chuckles. "Adeline and I have talked about having a destination wedding, but we don't know where."

"I wouldn't mind that either. But apparently, Vegas is off the table." Kyle rolls his eyes, referring to yesterday's conversation with Sarah.

The bartender returns with our order, and we all take a sip of our drinks.

"So, Kevin," Andre says, getting my attention. "Are you dating anyone right now?"

I almost choke on my beer. He seems aware that something is going on between Monique and me, and I have a feeling he's digging for more information.

"Uh, no," I reply before taking another sip of beer.

"Really, dude?" Kyle looks at me as if he doesn't believe me. "You don't have the bitches lined up back in Seattle?"

I roll my eyes and shake my head. "No. I don't have any *women* lined up back in Seattle."

"Is there anyone you're interested in?" Andre asks, digging deeper.

I look over at him. He raises an eyebrow as if to let me know he *knows.* I shake my head.

"What about Monique?" Kyle asks, taking me by surprise. *Does he know, too?* "You two have been hanging out a lot on this trip."

I shrug, trying to play it off as nothing. "So... we're old friends. And we're the only single ones here with all you lovey-dovey couples."

Kyle nudges me with his elbow. "I've seen the way you

two look at each other. There's something there. Don't lie to us."

I'm speechless. Have Monique and I done a terrible job at hiding our fling?

"Yeah, you have hung out a lot," Andre says. "You were even together early this morning on Monique's porch when Adeline and I saw you."

"Oh, is that right?" Kyle turns to me. "Are you sure there's nothing you want to tell us?"

I shake my head and take another sip. Honestly, I would *love* to tell them about Monique and me, but that wouldn't be right. We agreed to keep our fling a secret, and I'm not the type of guy to kiss and tell.

"When we saw him with Monique this morning," Andre tells Kyle, "he was wearing the same clothes he had on yesterday."

My head whips toward them, and they both look at me. *Shit!*

Kyle laughs. "Oh, little brother. *Do* tell. Tell us the truth about you and Monique."

"Nothing's going on," I lie. "We're just friends. I was only wearing the same clothes this morning because I woke up early to see the sunrise and threw on the first things I found."

They both look at me, not saying a word.

"That's the truth," I say, trying to convince them.

"Okay," Kyle says. "I guess that kiss I saw you two share was nothing then."

"*What?* Where?" I ask, shocked that he saw us. My heart pounds in my chest. What did he see?

"You saw them kiss?" Andre asks.

"Sure did," Kyle says, taking a sip of his Bloody Mary.

Shaking my head, I figure I might as well explain things to them. Fuck. I guess Monique and I weren't as careful as we thought.

"Okay, look. Monique and I have been having fun while we're here in Belize. But we're just friends. That's it."

Kyle's head whips toward me. "You mean it's true? I just made the kiss up to see what you'd say!"

The blood drains from my face.

Andre laughs. "Oh my God. This is hilarious!"

Yeah, no, it's not. This is *not* hilarious. I fell for my brother's trick and divulged the truth about Monique and me. *Fuck!*

"Dude! Congrats," Kyle says, offering me a fist bump. "Monique is *hot.*"

I've never wanted to punch my brother in the face as much as I do right now.

But I won't cause a scene.

"Are you fucking kidding me right now?" I say, my voice lowered so I don't attract attention.

Kyle lowers his hand that I refuse to fist bump. "Whoa. Sorry, man. Didn't mean to ruffle your feathers." He rolls his eyes.

"Look. Monique and I are friends. We're enjoying each other's company in Belize. That's it, okay? Don't tell anybody else, though. We don't want our parents to find out and things to get complicated."

"Your secret's safe with me," Andre says. "But just so you know, Adeline is suspicious, too."

Great.

I look at Kyle, hoping he'll give me his word to stay quiet. He puts both hands up as if he's surrendering. "I won't say anything. Okay? Jeez."

We're all quiet for a moment before Andre speaks up again. "Can I just say one thing?"

I look at him and shrug my shoulders. "Go ahead."

"Adeline and I both think you two would make a great couple. She knows her sister well and hasn't seen her this happy and carefree in a long time. Maybe ever. She thinks you have something to do with that."

I don't know what to say.

Andre looks at me pointedly. "Don't tell her I told you that."

I nod. "I won't."

His words hit me hard. Monique appears happier than her sister's ever seen? Is that really because of me or because she's on vacation?

I take a swig of my beer. Maybe Monique and I need to talk about what will happen between us *after* our blissful time in Belize ends.

9

MONIQUE

After browsing through all the shops Placencia has to offer, Mom, Kathy, Sarah, Adeline, and I end up at the Tipsy Tuna for a late lunch. It's an outside bar with a beautiful view of the beach. There's music playing, and signs with funny sayings hang everywhere, such as "Warning: Consuming alcohol may make you believe you're whispering. We promise you're not" and "We have mixed drinks about feelings."

The five of us have had a fun day so far. We all bought a few souvenirs to take home with us. My favorite is a sheer pink scarf with a flower pattern. I'll be able to wear it in so many other ways than just as a scarf. It's long enough to wrap around and wear as a shirt in several ways. Adeline and Sarah bought ones in different colors after I showed them how versatile it can be.

After we order our drinks with chips and salsa, Mom, Kathy, and Sarah excuse themselves to use the restroom.

As soon as they're out of earshot, Adeline turns to me and asks, "What's going on between you and Kevin?"

Her sudden question makes me choke on my own saliva. "I'm sorry... what?"

"Come on, Monique. This morning when we saw the two of you together, he was

still wearing the same clothes he had on yesterday. Did he spend the night with you?"

I don't know what to say. I shake my head. "No... he just came over—"

"Monique," Adeline says in a knowing tone, "I'm not dumb. The two of you have been hanging out and giving each other googly eyes all week. You seem happier than you've been in a long time. What's up?"

I can't believe she knows, but at the same time I can. Adeline and I have always had a sisterly intuition with each other. There's no use in lying to her. Not only that, it will feel good to get this secret off my chest. I know I can trust her.

I turn my head toward the restroom to make sure no one is coming back yet, then I turn back to Adeline. "Okay. Fine. Yes, he stayed the night. Yes, we've been hooking up since we've been in Belize."

Adeline's hands fly to her mouth, and she squeals with excitement. "Oh my God! This is exciting!"

"Shh," I say, although I'm not sure why. No one we know is around to hear her. "It's just a fling."

She lowers her hands. "So what's going to happen when you go home? Will you keep in touch with him?"

I shrug. "I don't know. We haven't talked about it yet."

"Well... don't you think you should? I mean, you don't exactly live close to one another."

Thanks for pointing out the obvious, Sis.

"It's just a fling. Nothing serious."

She cocks an eyebrow. "How many times have the two of you hooked up?"

"I don't know... like two or three times, I guess..." *Downplay the situation!*

"Do you have feelings for him?"

Her question takes me by surprise. Yes, I have feelings for Kevin. But what do those feelings mean?

"Look. We're friends, and we've known each other our entire lives. Of course I have feelings for Kevin, but it's not as if I'm falling in love with him or anything."

As I say those words aloud, I realize they're not entirely true, though. Sure, we've only been hooking up, but my feelings for Kevin have grown. I'm not in love with him... but I could see myself falling for him if our relationship continued.

"Sometimes the best relationships start as friendships," Adeline says. "That's how Andre and I started out. I didn't want to admit I was falling for him at first, but the more we hung out together as friends, the more my feelings grew. Now... here we are, engaged."

I turn my head and see Mom, Kathy, and Sarah walking back to our table. "Look. I like him, but we're just having fun. Don't get all excited about this, and *don't* tell anyone," I say just before the three of them return.

Adeline gives me a knowing look as they all sit down, and that's the end of that conversation.

Damn! If Adeline knows, does that mean Andre knows, too? Does anyone else? I didn't think we were that obvious, but maybe we are.

Crap.

And I realize that Kevin and I should probably discuss what's going to happen in two days when we both fly home, but at the same time, I don't want to. I want to live in this Belize bliss while I still can—no strings, no commitment, just a fun time with an old friend.

However, I know how much I'm going to miss Kevin. Maybe that's the real reason I'm avoiding that conversation. What *is* going to happen between us once our vacation is over? Will we keep in touch? Will it be another decade before we see each other again? The thought of that feels like a knife twisting in my gut. I like Kevin—*a lot* —and after spending these past few days together, I want him to be in my life.

But how realistic is that? I own a business in Paris. He lives in Seattle. Sure, we could visit each other, but traveling abroad gets expensive. I need to be realistic about this situation so my heart doesn't get broken in the end.

"What time should we leave for Xunantunich in the morning?" Dan consults my dad as we all discuss tomorrow's excursion to the Mayan ruins.

"It's over a three-hour drive, so we should leave early. Does nine o'clock sound good?"

"Sounds good to me," Dan says, then turns to the rest

of us sitting at the dinner table at The Bistro. "Everyone be ready to leave by nine tomorrow morning."

We all agree, although a three-hour drive does not sound intriguing at all. Sure, seeing ancient Mayan ruins sounds exciting, but I didn't realize we'd have to travel across the country to see them.

After dinner, everyone walks out on the beach again. I can't believe tomorrow is the last night I'll be able to enjoy this view before heading home. I'm going to miss this. Not only is it beautiful here but I've also had the best vacation of my life. I've been able to detach from work and enjoy myself. I left my boutique in good hands with Becca, so I know I have nothing to worry about. She would've called me if she had any issues, and she hasn't. I've only texted her twice—once when I arrived here, and once yesterday when she texted to ask how I was enjoying my trip.

I look at Kevin, walking with his parents. I'm so attracted to him, I can hardly stand it. I'm not looking forward to saying goodbye. Hopefully, we'll have the chance to be together at least a couple of more times. We have tonight and tomorrow night left in Belize, and if I have my way, we'll spend them both together.

We all say good night to one another in front of the building that houses everyone's hotel rooms but Kevin's and mine. As I give Adeline a hug, she whispers in my ear, "Have fun tonight."

She winks at me as we pull apart. She's never going to let this go. I'll probably get text messages from her for the next several months asking what's going on between Kevin and me. *Great*—just what I need.

After everyone heads toward their rooms, Kevin and I are left alone. We start walking toward our huts.

"Did you have a good day?" he asks.

"Yeah. Did you?"

"Yeah, I did. Kyle actually behaved himself today, so that was nice."

"That's good. He can be a handful."

He doesn't reply to that. He's quiet for a moment before he says, "Andre and Kyle both know about us."

I stop dead in my tracks. "What?"

Kevin stops and turns toward me. "Earlier today, Andre started grilling me about being on your porch this morning. Then Kyle joined in. I denied anything was going on between us, but then Kyle said he saw us kissing..."

Kyle saw us? When?

Kevin continues. "But it turns out he just made that up to get me to confess... which unfortunately worked. So... yeah. I'm sorry."

I don't know what to say. I can't be mad at Kevin. After all, I told Adeline the truth about us, too. I suppose I should come clean and let him know that.

I rub my forehead, then reply, "It's okay. Adeline knows, too."

The corners of Kevin's mouth lift a fraction as if he's relieved. "She does?"

"Yeah. The same thing happened to me at lunch today. Adeline and I were alone
at the table while the others were in the bathroom, and she grilled me about you. I ended up confessing that we've been hooking up."

Kevin smiles. "I guess the cat's out of the bag."

"I guess so," I reply. "Sarah doesn't know, though, and neither do our moms."

"Well, that's good," he says as we begin walking again. "Neither do our dads."

I laugh. "My dad would probably kill you."

"He would? But your dad likes me!"

"But I'm his little girl... his *ma fille chérie*," I explain. "What dad wants to find out that their daughter is having sex?"

"True." We approach Kevin's hut and stop walking.

"Can you imagine what our moms would do if they found out?"

He laughs. "I guarantee my mom would *not* want to kill you."

"That's true. Your mom loves me. Our moms would probably start planning our wedding if they knew." I laugh.

But Kevin's not laughing. He's looking at me in a way I haven't seen before. His eyes are soft and sultry but also sad. I wonder what he's thinking, but looking at him now watching me this way, I don't want to talk anymore.

I throw myself into him, wrapping my arms around his neck and kissing him hard on the lips. His strong arms wrap around me, holding me close, his hands caressing my back. "Your room," I say between kissing his soft lips. "Now."

To my utter shock, Kevin lifts me off the ground, picking me up to carry me to his room. I wrap my legs around his waist, and we continue kissing as he skillfully walks us up to the porch of his hut. When we get to the door, he gently sets me down, letting my body slide down the front of his. He quickly unlocks the door, then we hurry inside.

"God, I want you," he says, locking the door behind him.

I lift my shirt over my head and drop it to the floor as he stalks toward me. "I need you," I say right before he crashes his lips to mine again.

Fumbling with the waistband of his shorts, I manage to pull them down. To my surprise, he's not wearing any underwear. I wrap my hand around his cock, and his lips pull away from mine as he looks down at the contact.

"Fuck, that's hot," he says, watching as I stroke him. "That feels so good. Don't stop, baby."

He looks back up again and kisses me hard. I glide my hand up and down his rigid length, and I know it's driving him wild when he moans. Knowing how much I affect him is a total turn-on for me.

All of a sudden, he steps back a fraction, and I drop my hand. "Take off your clothes and get on the bed," he says as he pulls his shirt over his head. "I need to be inside you. Now."

His words send a thrill through my body, and I do what he says. After peeling the rest of my clothing off, I crawl onto the bed and lie back against the pillows. Kevin finishes undressing and slides a condom onto his dick before joining me on the bed. He braces himself above me and looks me in the eyes, softly brushing my cheek. My belly muscles clench as I look into his blue eyes, feeling adored by this man.

Without a word, I spread my legs farther apart, and he presses the head of his cock against my wet core. His lips press to mine as he pushes inside, sinking as deep as he can go. I moan, wrapping my legs around his waist. He slides deeper, hitting that deep spot that stings with pleasure, and then he rears back before plunging deep again.

Kevin and I move together at a steady pace, pushing both of us closer to release. He rolls us over so I have control, and I ride his cock, swiveling my hips in a way that feels amazing. My first orgasm rips through me, and I moan loudly.

"That's right, baby," Kevin says as my muscles continue to contract. "You're going to make me come so hard."

But he doesn't come yet. He lasts longer as I continue to fuck him, and then he rolls us over so he's on top once more. He pounds into me and increases his pace, causing me to come undone seconds before he lets out a guttural moan and pours himself into me.

Sex with Kevin seems to get better and better every time we do it. I don't want to think about the limited time we have left together here. I wish our circumstances could be different. With only one more day to spend in Belize, I vow to make the most of our time together... at least, the best I can while still keeping our fling a secret from our parents.

10

KEVIN

"**T**his is the ferry boat we have to take?" Kyle asks the question I'm sure is going through all our minds.

Ahead of us is basically a flat, covered, wooden raft, which is connected to a hand-cranked rope pulley system that takes one car at a time across the Mopan River. It's the only way to get to the Xunantunich Mayan ruins. Dad pulls forward in line, and one of the ferry workers approaches the driver's side. Dad rolls down the window to talk to the man.

"Hello!" the jovial man says in his Belizean accent. "Please full forward onto the

ferry and park in the center. Everyone but the driver will need to exit the vehicle and stand on the ferry as we cross."

"Oh really?" Mom says, surprised by this news.

"Yes, ma'am. For safety."

Kyle leans over and murmurs, "What the fuck?"

I shrug. This seems sketchy, but Dad doesn't seem bothered by it. He pulls forward onto the ferry, where another guy directs him where to park in the middle. Then Mom, Sarah, Kyle, and I get out of the car and stand on the wooden platform. I look behind us and see the Blanchets' SUV waiting in line to go after we cross. I wave, but with the reflections on the windshield, I can't tell if they're waving back.

A man cranks the ferry's mechanism, and we start moving across the river. This is unbelievable. I've never seen anything like this before, and I quickly take my phone out and begin taking pictures.

Pictures. It occurs to me that Monique and I haven't taken any pictures together on this trip. We've been so secretive about our fling, it never occurred to me to take any selfies with her. There have been a few photos with everyone in both our families involved, but nothing with just the two of us. The realization makes me sad. I want to have a memento of our time together in Belize. Something to capture our amazing time here. I need to take a picture of us today.

The ferry reaches the other side, and one of the men instructs Dad to drive off, then he can park and wait for us. We have to walk off the boat, then we can get back in the car. We still have to drive up a gravel road in order to get to the ruins, which are up a hill about a mile or so.

The four of us get back into the SUV with Dad. "I'm going to wait for the Blanchets to cross," he says, so we sit and wait for them. Luckily, it's a short trip on the ferry, and it's not long before we're on our way again.

It's a short drive up the hill to the parking lot and entrance to the ruins. We park, and the Blanchets park next to us. We all get out of the car, and Monique and I make eye contact right away. I smile as thoughts of last night come flooding back. I can't believe our week in Belize is ending, and Monique and I only have one more night to spend together.

I'm really going to miss her.

We all head toward the ticket booth to pay our entrance fees. We still can't see the ruins from where we're at, though. After getting our tickets, we have to walk up another hill to the site. Monique and I fall to the back of our group and walk side by side.

"What'd you think of the drive here?" I ask her.

"It was... interesting. Belize is a beautiful country, that's for sure. It's just unbelievable how you'll see beautiful homes, but down the road are shacks that look as if a strong wind could knock them down."

"I know what you mean," I reply. "The poverty in this country is real... although everyone who lives here still seems happy."

"I guess that goes to show that money can't buy happiness."

"Yes," I agree. "That's definitely true."

As we approach the top of the hill, the first ruin comes into view. Everyone stops walking when we get to it, and we see others scattered all around. This site is much larger than I thought it would be.

"This is amazing," Mom says, looking around at all of the structures we can see just from where we're standing.

"There's so much to see. I guess we don't all have to stick together," Dad says.

"I'd like to get a picture of all of us in front of the largest ruin, though," Mom replies. "So everyone, let's meet in front of it in about thirty minutes."

We all agree, then start to walk in different directions. Monique and I don't move, though. Instead, we turn and look at one another.

"Would you like to walk around together?" she asks, and I'm grateful for her suggestion.

"I was going to ask you the same thing," I reply. "I'd love to."

We start walking, looking at all the temples surrounding us. Neither of us says anything as we take in the impressive tall buildings made of stone that have been standing since about 600 AD. It's mind-blowing to think how long these structures have been here. Each of us snaps a few photos on our phones, and I decide this is a good opportunity to get a selfie together.

"Come take a picture with me," I say.

She turns toward me and smiles. "Okay."

She walks over and stands at my side. No one else we know is within view, so I put my arm around her. Holding my phone up, I snap a couple of pictures of us. I don't even care if I get the temple behind us in the shot. I just want a photo of us.

After snapping the photos, I lower my arm, then turn to face her. We're in a semi-secluded area, so I take the opportunity to kiss her sweet lips. Luckily, she doesn't object. She leans into me, wrapping her arms around me and kissing me with all she's got. I shove my phone in my back pocket to free my hands, then run my fingers through her hair. I suck her tongue in my mouth, then relinquish dominance to her. She lightly bites my lip before we hear a rustling sound and quickly pull away from each other.

We turn to see what made the sound, but we don't see anyone.

"Maybe it was a bird," I say, hoping that was the case and not someone in our family who saw us kissing.

"You'll have to send that to me," she says.

"I will."

We hear the sound again, and I notice what it is this time. "Holy crap. That's a big lizard!"

I walk toward the lizard, and she follows. "What? Where?"

"Right there," I say, pointing at the large, scaly creature only a few feet away from us. "I think it's a green iguana. I've heard they live here."

"Oh my gosh! That's so cool!"

I look at Monique, who's looking at the lizard with childlike wonder. She takes her phone out again to capture a photo of the wild creature. I take my phone out of my pocket as well, but I don't snap a photo of the iguana. Instead, I take a couple of candid photos of Monique. She's absolutely beautiful, and I want to remember this moment —our last day in Belize, seeing a green iguana together right after sharing a hot kiss.

I'm suddenly filled with a heavy feeling that I don't like. My heart's in my throat. I don't want to say goodbye to her tomorrow.

"Hey, guys!" Kyle's voice comes from behind me, and I turn to see him and Sarah walking toward us. "What are you looking at?"

"It's an iguana," I say, pointing at the animal who's sitting still in the same spot. We've probably scared the poor guy.

"Whoa," Kyle says when he spots the lizard. "I thought iguanas were small lizards people kept as pets."

I chuckle. "Well, that's true, but there are different kinds."

Sarah looks freaked out and stands behind Kyle. "Do-do those things attack?" she asks.

I shake my head, but Monique replies before I can. "No, they're harmless," she says. "At least, I think they are... this one has just been sitting here the whole time we've been taking pictures of it."

"I wonder if I can pick it up," Kyle says.

I panic as he moves closer. Is he really that stupid?

"No!" Sarah screeches, pulling on Kyle's arm. "Don't do that! He'll bite you!"

Kyle stops, and I take the opportunity to intervene. "Yeah, man, I wouldn't try. They have sharp claws, and he'll probably fuck you up."

Even Monique pipes up. "And it might have diseases."

Kyle considers what we're saying, then concedes. "Okay, fine. I won't. But wouldn't it be cool if I did?" He laughs.

I chuckle once to humor him. "Yeah. For sure. But you shouldn't do it."

"Let's go over here," Sarah suggests, pointing at another structure.

Kyle slips his hand in hers and agrees. "See you two later," he says to Monique and me as they walk away.

Once they're out of earshot, Monique says quietly, "I can't believe your brother."

"Neither can I," I say, shaking my head. "Can you imagine what could've happened if we didn't stop him?"

Suddenly, we hear leaves rustling and turn to see the lizard scurrying away.

"That was really cool," Monique says. "I'm glad I got to witness that with you."

That heavy feeling appears again. Monique and I have such a limited time left together, and we still haven't talked about what'll happen once we both go home. I suppose now is as good a time as any...

"So I've been meaning to ask you," I say, deciding to bring up the tough conversation now while we have a moment alone.

Monique's sparkling hazel eyes look up into mine with anticipation.

"Do you want to keep in touch after we leave tomorrow? I know we don't live anywhere near each other, but—"

"Yes," she says before I can even finish my sentence. "I want to stay in touch with you, Kevin."

She smiles sweetly, and the heavy feeling lightens up a little. "I'm glad you said that," I reply, relieved. "I wish we didn't have to say goodbye tomorrow."

She looks down for a moment, then back up at me,

although the smile has faded from her face. "I feel the same way."

We just look at one another, holding each other's gaze for I don't know how long. I have so many things I want to say to her right now, but I can't say them. I can't tell her that I wish we could continue our fling... that I wish we could spend more time together back home... that I wish we lived in the same city so I could take her out on dates and get to know her better. I'll always cherish our time together in Belize, but it doesn't seem like enough. I feel as if our relationship could turn into so much more. I could have a *real* relationship with Monique... I can see us being together for real, without having to hide it from our families.

Fuck. I can't say any of that out loud to her, but I wonder what she's thinking. Does she feel the same way, or is she looking forward to being distant friends, thousands of miles apart, who only speak on occasion?

The sound of footsteps interrupts our silent moment, and we both turn to see Adeline and Andre walking nearby. They see us and wave, but continue on their way.

"We should go look at the rest of the site," Monique says. "There's still a lot to see."

"Yeah, let's go," I agree, swallowing hard. I don't like this feeling I have. Sure, we've agreed to stay in touch, but to what extent?

When it's time, we meet everyone in front of the largest structure, which is called El Castillo. I can't imagine how difficult it must've been for the Mayans to carry all of these heavy stones and put them into place, especially with how tall this temple is.

"Okay, let's stand close together," Mom says, instructing everyone as she looks at her phone to ensure the photo will turn out great. She's asked another visitor to take our photo, who's standing next to her, waiting for us to be ready.

We quickly arrange ourselves, and I find myself standing behind Monique. No one can see, so I take the opportunity to place my hand on her ass. Her head whips around to look at me in surprise, and I smile at her. She giggles, silently as to not attract anyone else's attention, then quickly turns around to face the camera again. Mom is in place next to dad, and the stranger snaps a few photos for us. Once she's done, she hands the phone back to Mom, who hurries over to retrieve her phone and thank the lady.

Xunantunich is incredible, and I'm glad we took the long drive to see it. I also enjoyed the time I got to spend with Monique today. As Dad drives us back to Placencia, Mom suddenly holds a picture on her phone up for me to see. "Look at this! You and Monique look like you're laughing at something."

I look at the photo and see it was the moment I grabbed Monique's ass and she turned to look at me. We're smiling at each other and look... happy. Like we're sharing a special moment together.

Kyle nudges my arm with his. "Cute pic," he says. "You two would make a cute couple."

I glare at my brother, who just gives me a knowing

smile. Mom isn't paying attention to us, though, and takes her phone back. "I'll send that to you," she says.

"Thanks," I reply with a chuckle, trying to laugh it off so Mom doesn't suspect anything.

Kyle shakes his head with a cocky grin on his face. I nudge him with my elbow. "Ow," he says. "What the hell?"

I give him a pointed look, not wanting to say anything out loud, afraid our parents will hear. It feels like we're kids again, not wanting to get in trouble as we have an argument in the back seat of the car. Luckily, Sarah steals Kyle's attention by showing him a picture she took on her phone, and he doesn't bother me any more about it.

When we finally make it back to the Maya Beach Hotel, it's dinnertime and we're all hungry. All of us, including the Blanchets, head straight to The Bistro. It's our last dinner in Belize, and I'm going to splurge and get the grilled lobster tail meal.

And I don't regret it. The food is delicious, just as it's been every time we've eaten at The Bistro on this trip. I'm going to miss eating here.

After dinner, we all take a stroll on the beach, then end up in Mom and Dad's hotel room, making drinks to use up the rest of the bottles of alcohol that we bought over the course of the week but can't take back to the States. It's a fun night, hanging out with my family and the Blanchets. This is a perfect way to end our vacation. Reflecting on the past week, I realize how special it's been to spend this valuable time with my parents and Kyle. I've had the opportunity to get to know his fiancée a little more, too. I'll always treasure this time with my family. It really has been an incredible vacation, and I feel lucky to be able to come here.

And Monique. Damn. I feel like the luckiest man alive to have been able to spend the time with her that I did. She's an incredible woman, and I'll always treasure the time we had together as well.

As the evening gets later and the alcohol bottles get emptier, I have a happy buzz going on, as does everyone else, as far as I can tell. Monique's parents say good night to everyone and head to their room, followed by Adeline and Andre a short time later. After that, Kyle and Sarah announce they're leaving, and then Monique does, too. That's my cue—I want to leave with her. This is our last night together, and if I have my way, we'll spend it together.

I say good night to my parents, giving them hugs, and Monique does as well. It feels like we're a couple leaving together, just like everyone else who left as a couple. A guy can dream, right?

Monique and I leave my parents' room and head toward our huts.

"Do you want to go out on the dock?" she asks. "I want to savor this last night in Belize."

"Sure. I'll follow you."

Monique and I make our way out to the covered dock. Aside from the hotel's lights and the light on the dock, it's completely dark outside. No one is out and about walking on the beach, and no one else is on the dock. Monique and I are all alone.

She sits on the bench swing, so I sit next to her.

"You still need to send me the selfie you took of us earlier," she says.

"Oh right," I reply, taking my phone out of my pocket. "I need your phone number."

It's crazy to think I don't have her contact info, but there hasn't been a reason for us to exchange it yet. It's not as if we've needed our phones to get in touch with each other while we've been here.

"So... it costs more to text someone overseas. Are you on social media? We can keep in contact that way," she says.

I hadn't even considered that before. Just another hurdle of living so far apart.

"Yeah, I am. Are you on Insta?" I ask, opening the app.

"Yep. I'm Monique, underscore, Lavender, underscore, Lace," she says.

I type her name into the search bar and find her right away. Her profile pic is a beautiful photo of her, and I recognize the background. "Did you take this here?" I ask, noticing the turquoise water and covered dock in the background.

She nods. "Yeah, I did. My first day here."

"You look gorgeous." It's the truth. She's absolutely stunning.

"Thank you," she says. "That's sweet of you."

I hit the follow button, then look at her account. The recent pictures are of Belize, but as I scroll through, I see photos of her shop, Lavender Lace. "Your shop looks nice. I bet people love shopping there."

"Thanks. I'm pretty proud of it." She looks at her phone and opens the app. "I'll follow you back."

Within a few seconds, I get the notification that Monique followed me.

"You don't post a lot." She laughs. "You only have like ten pictures."

I shrug. "I don't have that many interesting things to post about."

"Well, now you do. You can post some pics from Belize."

"True. I'll do that when I get back home."

We put our phones down and sit in silence for a moment, looking out at the dark water that lies in front of us. The sound of the waves is the only thing we hear. It's peaceful, and I want to commit this last night in Belize with Monique to memory.

"I'm going to miss you." Monique's voice cuts through the silence, taking me by surprise.

I turn my head to look at her. "I'm going to miss you, too." I might as well be completely honest.

Some strands of hair fall in front of her face, so I reach up and brush them back. Before I can say another word about how much I'll miss her, she presses her lips to mine. I moan at the contact. One thing's for sure, I thoroughly enjoy kissing Monique, and I want to do it as much as possible before we leave tomorrow.

Our tongues lash together before she suddenly breaks away. She gets up from the swing and kneels in front of me, her hands on my thighs. She looks up at me through her lashes, and I have a feeling I know what she's going to do, which is a complete turn-on.

Monique's hands deftly undo the fly of my shorts. I adjust the way I'm sitting to allow her easier access as her hand dips inside my boxer briefs, reaching for my shaft. "You don't have to do this here," I say. "We can go back to your room... or mine."

"I want to do this here," she says, stroking my cock from the base to the tip. "I've wanted to do this with you here... It's a little naughty... and hot."

And with that, she wraps her lips around my cock, taking me deep in her warm, wet mouth.

My head falls back, and I outstretch my arms along the back of the swing. I have a feeling this is just the beginning of a very enjoyable evening with Monique.

11

MONIQUE

After spending all day with Kevin, looking like the fine sex on a stick he is, I can't help myself. Sucking his cock on the covered dock, knowing someone could walk out here and see us at any moment, excited me so much I had to do it. Chances are low that anyone will actually see us, but the danger of it all turns me on. Of course, I don't want to finish him off out here, though... I want to pleasure him for a bit, then take him back to my room where we can continue our last night and finish together.

Kevin groans as I suck him, sliding my mouth up and down his length. My tongue presses the underside of his cock as I slide upward, and he growls. "Fuck, baby. That feels good."

Baby. I love the way it sounds when he calls me that. My belly muscles clench, and I know we can't stay out here too much longer. I need more.

Kevin's hand tangles in my hair as I continue sucking him. "Monique," he says, his voice shaky, "I want to be inside you. Let's go back to your hut."

I ignore his request for a moment and continue bobbing up and down on his cock. I look up at him and see the sexiest sight—Kevin's eyes are closed, and he looks as if he's in ecstasy.

However, the ache between my legs increases, and I can't wait much longer. I go down on him again, his head hitting the back of my throat, sliding my mouth back up, then off, making a popping sound as I pull my mouth away with one final suck.

"Damn," Kevin says as I stand and take his hand. "That was incredible."

"Let's go to my room," I say, pulling his hand so he'll stand and go with me.

Which is exactly what he does after he quickly zips his shorts up. We walk hand in hand back to my hut. Walking with him like this feels good, not worrying about anyone in our families seeing us since we know they're all in their rooms for the night. I wish we could've had more moments like this, walking together with his hand in mine. His hand seems to fit mine like a glove.

We're all over each other as soon as we're in my room with the door shut and the curtains closed. It doesn't take long to undress one another, and before I know it, I'm lying on the bed with Kevin settling between my legs, his head at the apex of my thighs. I spread my legs apart, and he dives right in, swiping his tongue against my bundle of nerves.

"Oh my God," I say, enjoying the pleasure. I close my eyes, and Kevin inserts a finger, sliding it in and out of my pussy as he licks my clit.

I reach down, sliding my fingers through his hair.

"Your pussy's so sweet," he says before going right back to licking me.

Between his finger and his tongue, it doesn't take long for that familiar tingling feeling to start, and I know I'm going to come. "Yes!" I call out as my orgasm rips through me, and I grip his hair, giving it a tug.

"Mmm," he moans. "You're so sexy when you come."

As I begin to relax, I release his hair. Kevin moves swiftly, retrieving a condom and sheathing his cock before climbing back on the bed. I look up into his blue eyes as he lines himself up, ready to slide into my wet pussy. But he doesn't push inside me yet. Instead, he carefully smoothes the hair out of my face and looks at me—dare I say —lovingly.

"You're so beautiful, Monique," he says. "I'm going to miss you so much."

My heart pounds rapidly in my chest. His words make me feel wanted, and I wish we didn't have to say goodbye tomorrow. The thought that this could be our last time ever sleeping together crosses my mind, and it's like a punch to the gut. It makes me sad to think about, so instead, I wrap my hand around his neck, pull his head down, and kiss his delectable lips.

Kevin and I kiss, the passion exploding between us as our tongues volley back and forth. His cock presses against my pussy, and he pushes inside, going all the way to the hilt. I moan because it feels so good. As he moves back and forth, my arms wrap around him, wanting to keep him close.

This could be our last time.

I grind my hips against him, and he pushes in deeper. "Yes!" I hiss, clawing at his back.

We might never see each other again.

I want this to last as long as possible. "I wanna ride you," I say, hoping he'll roll over and let me be on top so he lasts longer.

He grants my wish and rolls us over, not breaking our precious contact. I sit up and move up and down his cock. It feels even better for me in this position, and I know I'll come again soon.

This is the best sex I've ever had.

"You're so fucking sexy," Kevin says, watching me ride him. "Come on my cock. I wanna feel you come on me."

His words are my undoing, and I come apart, calling out in pleasure.

I'm going to miss this.

Kevin rolls us back over and starts moving at a steady pace. I look up at him and see he's watching me. "You feel so good. Your pussy's so wet," he says before kissing me again. His hands caress my body as we move together, our tongues gliding back and forth.

He's everything I want in a partner.

Fuck! I need to block all these thoughts that keep popping in my head and just enjoy this last night with Kevin. I'm afraid the feelings I already have for him are growing, and that's not what I need now. We're about to go our separate ways, and I have no idea if I'll see him again in the near future... and by *near future,* I mean within the next decade or so.

His cock fills me, hitting me deep, driving me wild. It doesn't take long before I come again, calling out Kevin's name as I do.

This can't be it. I need more with him!

Selfishly, I don't want this to end yet. "Let me ride you again," I say, hoping he'll agree, and he does.

Kevin rolls us over so I can have my turn at fucking him again. I lean over and kiss him hard on the lips as I move my hips up and down.

"Slower," he says. "I don't wanna come yet."

Oh. He wants this to last, too.

I slow my movements. It still feels incredible to me, and even going slow, I know it won't take me long to get there again. But as I look at Kevin, I see him watching me with adoration in his eyes. He's feeling something, too, and I'm suddenly overwhelmed with a warm feeling.

He touches my face. "I don't want to say goodbye," he says before kissing me again.

"Neither do I." I swirl my hips, and the motion sets me off. My body erupts in another intense orgasm.

No man has ever given me so much pleasure before.

Tomorrow's going to be hell.

I don't want tonight to end.

Kevin takes control and rolls us over once more. He calls out my name as he eventually comes inside me, setting off another orgasm for me.

We lie in each other's arms, completely satisfied. I
listen to his heart beating in his chest, and it's synced with
the beating of mine. At this moment, I feel more connected
to Kevin than ever, and I fear that my emotions are
heading into that scary L-word territory.

No. I am not *falling in love with Kevin Blake!*

I refuse to let that thought set up camp in my brain.
Only one thing will happen if I ponder it for too long—my
heart will end up shattering into pieces, and I can't let that
happen.

"I don't want to leave," Kevin says out of the blue.
We've been lying together in silence for so long that I
wondered if he fell asleep.

"Then don't," I reply. "Spend the night with me."

"Okay," he agrees, then gives me a light squeeze and
kisses my forehead. "Monique?"

"Yeah?"

"I... I like you... a lot," he says, and my heart flutters.

"I like you a lot, too."

Like is okay... *like* I can handle. Sure, it will still hurt
like hell to say goodbye to Kevin, but this L-word isn't
nearly as scary and hurtful as the other one.

———

The next day, I wake up in Kevin's arms. I won't admit how
good it feels to sleep with him wrapped around me. The
memories we've made together will always be special to
me, and I'll look back on this trip with fondness in my
heart.

Kevin and I have sex again before getting out of bed, then he leaves to go back to his hut and get ready for the day. Meanwhile, I take a shower and get myself ready. I need to pack and get ready to go home, which I'm *not* looking forward to.

Everyone meets for breakfast at nine. We need to leave for the airport by ten thirty, and we all have a long day of travel ahead of us. Mine is the longest, though, and I'm not excited about the jet lag I'll endure once I'm back in Paris. I won't even arrive there until nine o'clock *tomorrow* morning. I have to fly from Belize City to Miami first, where I'll have to wait a couple of hours before boarding my flight to Paris.

This, of course, will all be after surviving the tiny plane ride from Placencia to Belize City this morning. All ten of us are on that flight, which means we may be the only passengers on that small plane. I believe there were about twelve seats in all.

Breakfast is enjoyable with everyone there. Kevin and I sit next to one another. Although we have to keep our hands to ourselves, being able to brush against him occasionally has its benefits.

God, I'm going to miss him!

When we get to the Placencia airport, we all pile inside the Tropic Air building, which is about the size of a large living room in a house. There's no security gate here. I guess they're not concerned about hijackers or terrorists getting onto one of their flights.

Sure enough, only two other passengers besides our large group await our flight. There's not a gate, per se, and when it's time to board the plane, an airline worker simply tells us and opens the door to let us out onto the tarmac. No need to recheck our tickets... there are only twelve of us, and they checked them a short time ago when we walked into the building.

Kevin and I walk beside each other, behind the rest of our family members. His hand brushes mine, and he actually takes hold of it. I look at him, surprised he's taking this chance with our families just a few feet away. He smiles, blows me a kiss, then releases my hand.

Instantly, I miss his touch.

We board the large roller skate, and Kevin and I find ourselves sitting in the last row behind everyone else. After we buckle our seat belts, he takes my hand in his again. I could get used to this. I *wish* I could get used to this. But it's over much too soon when his mom turns her head slightly and he lets go in fear of her seeing us.

As the plane takes off, though, he takes hold of it again. His touch helps me relax. Maybe this flight won't be so bad after all.

And it's not. The flight is smooth all the way to Belize City, and the views are spectacular. The blue waters of the Caribbean Sea sparkle in the sunlight. The different shades of green foliage over the land puts into perspective just how much jungle there is west of the beaches in Belize. I hope I have the chance to come back to this beautiful country again someday.

Kevin and I are sitting close enough that our hands touch in some way the entire flight. I have butterflies but also a bit of anxiety trying to enjoy this time with him. I wish we didn't have to hide it from everyone. I'd love to be able to lean my head on his shoulder or fully link our fingers together without worrying about someone turning around and seeing us. It's weird, but I'm actually looking forward to saying goodbye to him and getting on my flight to Paris.

In no way do I want to say goodbye to Kevin, but I have to move on with my life. I have no idea when, or even if, we'll see each other again. As our plane touches down in Belize City, a part of me wants to cut the cord quickly and say goodbye to Kevin as soon as possible. Prolonging our time together feels like a knife that continues to get twisted in my gut, and I want nothing more than for that feeling to go away.

Our plane comes to a stop, and they let us off. Kevin and I go back to behaving as friends, not a couple who spent the past several days hiding our relationship from everyone. Can I call what we had a relationship? I mean, we have a friendly relationship—a *very* friendly relationship—and hooked up every chance we got... so I guess we had some sort of a relationship together.

I have an hour layover here, but everyone else has to catch their flight to Denver in just a few minutes. With the airport being so small—although not nearly as small as the Placencia airport—I walk with them to their gate so I can say goodbye before they board their plane.

As we approach their gate, it's crowded with people lining up to board. It's a zoo, and my anxiety increases as I stand with my family and friends near the back of the line. Our backs are practically up against a wall here, but at least we have a space to stand. Since I'm the only one not flying to Denver with them, I'm the only one my family and the Blakes have to say goodbye to, and Kathy starts the goodbyes by giving me a sweet hug.

"It was so nice to see you, Monique," she says as she embraces me. "We'd love

to come to Paris someday for a visit."

"That would be wonderful," I say before we pull apart from each other.

Maybe Kevin can come with you.

Dan says goodbye to me next, followed by Sarah and Kyle. Kevin gives me the same sort of goodbye as the rest of his family, including a brief hug, and that's it. I'm craving to kiss his lips one more time, but that won't happen.

Next, my own family takes their turns saying goodbye to me, starting with Adeline and Andre. Of course, Adeline hugs me longer than anyone else has at this point. "I can't wait to see you again," she says in my ear. "I want you to be my maid of honor."

I give my little sister a squeeze. "Of course I'll be your maid of honor," I say, unexpectedly getting choked up at the thought.

Dad says goodbye to me next, followed by Mom, who says the longest goodbye, holding me as long as she can. When we finally pull away from each other, she wipes a tear from her eye, which makes me tear up as well. It's always difficult saying goodbye to my family, especially Mom.

The line moves as the flight begins to board. Just when

I think the goodbyes are done, Kevin announces, "I need to use the bathroom real quick."

"Kevin, you need to hurry," his mom says. "They're starting to board!"

"I'll be quick," he says before turning and giving me a subtle nod, motioning for me to follow him.

As soon as he starts to walk away, I say, "I need to use the restroom, too. I'll be right back."

"Monique!" Mom sounds frustrated. "Hurry back so I can hug you again before I board!"

The restrooms aren't far away, but they're around a corner, out of sight of our family members. I follow Kevin in that direction, but he walks past the men's room door and stops in a corner away from other people. As soon as I walk up to him, he pulls me into his arms and kisses me like his life depends on it.

My hands tangle in his hair, not wanting to release him. I don't want this kiss to end because it's likely our last. Once Kevin returns to Seattle, he'll go back to his life, and I'll return to mine in Paris. Sure, we'll keep in touch, but the distance will eventually grow between us. Although I wish our fate could be different, I know this is how it'll be.

Our tongues glide together, and I press my body against his, feeling his rigid length against my belly. I wish we weren't in a crowded airport right now. I'm sure passersby are thinking *get a room*, and believe me, I wish we could.

And then it all ends. Kevin reluctantly pulls his lips away, ending our fiery kiss. He peppers sweet kisses on my cheeks, my forehead, then the tip of my nose before he pulls back and looks at me. "I'm going to miss you."

A lump forms in my throat, and I have to push back the new tears forming in my eyes. "I'm going to miss you, too."

The second he releases me, I miss his touch. "I have to go," he says, and I swear he's holding back tears. Without another word, he heads back to the gate.

Fighting my own tears from falling, I follow a short distance behind him. Our families think we used the restrooms, after all, so I have to make that realistic.

This is so silly! I wish things didn't have to be this way.

When I return to the gate, Kevin, his family, and mine are almost to the ticket agent already. Mom sees me immediately and swiftly gives me another hug goodbye. Then Dad and Adeline each say goodbye to me again, too.

I stand to the side as the Blakes begin boarding. Before Kevin walks through the gate to leave, he gives me one final goodbye, waving to me and quickly blowing a kiss. Then he's gone.

Once my family boards, I'm left all alone. The airport is significantly less crowded now that all the people boarded the flight to Denver, and I notice the reggae Christmas music is playing over the sound system, just like it was when I arrived here last week.

My, how much has changed in a week. Yet some things are still the same. Like this music playing. I wonder how often this playlist has been on repeat since I was here last. I imagine it's been on a continuous cycle, playing in the background as people come and go through this terminal. All the while, I had a secret fling with Kevin, having the best sex of my life, making a connection with an old friend I never expected would happen in a million years. And now, although my life will return to the same as it was before arriving here in Belize, it's *not* the same. It's drastically different. I *feel* different.

I feel as if I'm missing a piece of my life.

12

MONIQUE

"Monique? Hello? Earth to Monique..." Becca waves her hand in front of my face, and I snap back to reality.

"Huh? What? I'm sorry." I shake my head and try to shake the memories of Kevin I was replaying in my head just now.

"I asked which dress you'd like me to put on the mannequin in the window," Becca says, holding up two of my new dress designs, one in each hand.

"Oh, umm..." I consider her question, trying to concentrate on the here and now, not Kevin's sexy face flashing through my brain. "Let's do that one," I say, pointing at the pale pink dress in her left hand.

"Okay, boss," she replies, then goes to put the other one away.

Once she walks away, I exhale. Kevin and I have communicated with each other multiple times a day, every day, for the past two weeks. I miss him. And I know he misses me because he tells me all the time. Neither of us knows when we'll be able to see each other again in person, though, and it's that unknown that makes the fact that we can't be together hurt even more.

I try to keep busy with work. That helps a little, but I also feel distracted more than I should be. Like what just happened with Becca, I'm not always paying attention when I need to be. Kevin is a distraction for me, and it's becoming a problem I didn't anticipate. I haven't been able to design any new clothing items since I've gotten back from Belize, and that's unusual for me. Instead of focusing my time on my career, Kevin is living rent free in my head.

I'm not sure how I feel about this. Sure, Kevin and I had something special in Belize, and I care about him deeply. But I can't let him distract me to the point that it's interfering with my job—my livelihood. I've worked hard to open my boutique and provide customers with quality clothes designed by me and other up-and-coming names in the industry. I *love* fashion, I *love* designing fashion, and I *love* helping others achieve their dreams of selling their designs in my store. I can't allow a man to come between me and my passion. I've worked too hard to make it this far, and I'm not about to let anyone or anything take that away from me.

My phone buzzes with a notification, and I see it's a message from Kevin. Considering he's nine hours behind me, he probably just woke up. I open the app to read his message.

Good morning, beautiful. I hope you're
having a good day.

"Hey, Mo?" Becca's voice sounds from the front of the store where she's dressing the mannequin.

"Yeah?" I holler back.

"Can you give me a hand?" she asks.

"Yep! Coming!" I walk to the front of the store and find her holding one of the mannequin's arms, detached from the rest of its body.

"What happened?" I ask, wondering how the mannequin broke.

"I don't know," she replies, looking at the arm in her hands. "It just popped off as I was undressing it, but I can't get it back on."

"Let me see," I say, and she hands me the arm. I evaluate the situation, taking a closer look at the arm and where it attaches to the mannequin. After some finagling, I'm finally able to reattach it. "There!"

"How'd you do that?" Becca asks. "I couldn't figure it out."

"I don't know. I just got lucky," I reply with a laugh.

"Well, thanks. Now I can get her dressed again," she says, moving toward it with the pale pink dress in her hands. "Hey, while you're here... are you okay? You seemed kinda dazed before."

I take a deep breath. "Yeah, I'm fine. Just a little distracted."

"Thinking about Kevin again?" she asks as she dresses the mannequin.

When I returned from Belize, I told Becca everything about Kevin and our fling.

"No..." I don't want to admit how much I think about him. If I do, then she might think my feelings for Kevin have grown exponentially, even with being thousands of miles apart. And that's absolutely *not* the case...

Or at least that's what I keep telling myself.

Becca looks at me, her eyes knitted in. She's not buying it.

I roll my eyes and concede. "Okay, fine. Yes, I was thinking about Kevin again."

She finishes dressing the mannequin, then brushes her hands together and

walks toward me. "It's okay to feel this way. You know I know exactly how you feel. I went through the same thing with Jack."

"I know. But at least things worked out for you and Jack. Kevin has no intention of leaving Seattle. I feel like it's a lost cause with him."

Becca looks at me sympathetically. "I'm sorry. Maybe things will change..."

I look down and shake my head. "I don't know."

Suddenly, a crash startles us both. We jump back and look in the direction of where the sound came from and see the mannequin's arm on the ground again.

"Well, crap!" I walk over and retrieve it off the tile floor. I inspect the dress to make sure it's not damaged, and it's fine. Then I try to reconnect the arm, but it's useless, so I finally give up. "I guess this is our new one-armed model."

Becca laughs. I take the arm to the back of the store to

put it in the storage room for now. Maybe I can fix it later, but I don't have the patience at the moment.

A thought comes to mind, and I don't like it. I find it ridiculous that I see a connection between a broken mannequin and my relationship with Kevin. There's a metaphor here, for sure. It's falling apart and broken with no fix in sight, and my patience is wearing thin.

Maybe Kevin and I can make things work someday when we both have the time to put into our relationship. Perhaps we can both be in the same time zone eventually. But for now, I'm feeling defeated.

Six months later

"You make such a beautiful bride," Mom gushes as she hugs Adeline, looking gorgeous in her white lace mermaid-style wedding dress.

"Thanks, Mom," Adeline beams. She looks happier than I've ever seen her before. She and Andre decided to have their wedding in Cancun, so our family is vacationing on the Caribbean Sea once again.

However, this setting is different from where we were in Belize. Here, we're staying at a large, all-inclusive resort that's crowded with people, as opposed to the small, quiet Maya Beach Hotel we stayed at in Placencia. My room isn't a beachside hut, but I'm not complaining about the beach view I have from my balcony on the ninth floor. Having a swim-up bar at the pool is a bonus, too, especially when all the drinks are included in the cost of our stay.

Adeline and Andre are having their wedding here at the resort, right on the beach. Only their closest friends and family are in attendance, including Kevin's parents...

But no Kevin.

It's hard to say exactly what happened between us. Feelings were strong when we first left Belize and returned to our homes. We kept in touch, and those feelings managed to hang on for both of us. However, the distance between us became a burden that weighed heavily on our hearts. After spending a couple of months talking multiple times a day, the messages we sent became fewer and fewer as time passed.

Then it happened.

Adeline and Andre's wedding invitations went out. They invited the entire Blake family. At first, Kevin said he wasn't sure if he could take the time off work to go... which didn't make sense to me since he works remotely. I was pissed, to say the least. This was our chance to finally see each other again, and he was making excuses not to? We argued and began talking even less to avoid fighting with each other.

Then he said he was, for sure, *not* going to the wedding. I was devastated. But the reason behind his decision made me even more upset. He said he *wanted* to see me. I was all he could think about, even when we were fighting. But he knew things would never work out between us, and he didn't want to see me only to have to say goodbye again. He said the best thing for us to do was go our separate ways for good.

He gave up on us.

And my heart broke into a million pieces.

From that moment, we stopped all communication with each other. I haven't heard from Kevin in nearly three months.

"Are you ready?" The wedding planner walks into the suite where all of us women in the bridal party are getting ready.

"Ready as I'll ever be," Adeline replies. She's glowing, and my heart swells with pride for my sister. Andre is her perfect match, and they'll be happy together.

The wedding planner, whose name is Mary, has all of us bridesmaids line up. I can't help but find the humor in her name being Mary, when her job is to help people get married. She's definitely good at what she does and has made everything run smoothly for Andre and Adeline.

Since I'm the maid of honor, I'm the last one in line, right in front of my sister. Mary hands out our bouquets, which are small bunches of pink hibiscus flowers. They go well with our light mint-green bridesmaid dresses. I like the dresses Adeline chose for us. After all, I designed them. In spite of the heartbreak I went through with Kevin, I still managed to do this for my sister. They're short, A-line dresses with spaghetti straps, and I added pockets to them for convenience.

I did not design her wedding dress, though. Since they had a short engagement, I didn't have enough time to do her dress in addition to ours. Plus, she found the one she wanted in a magazine she was looking through, and it truly is the perfect dress for her.

Mary leads us all outside in the direction of the ceremony. This is it—the big moment for my little sister and soon-to-be brother-in-law. Despite the heartache I've endured the past few months, I've been over the moon for Adeline.

I've also delivered an Oscar-worthy performance since arriving here in Cancun. Seeing Kevin's parents (Kyle and Sarah didn't come), as well as being in this tropical paradise that reminds me of Belize and my time with Kevin, has been excruciatingly hard. I've only cried once, though. Last night after hearing Dan and Kathy talk about what Kevin's been up to, I went back to my room and broke down. I can't show emotion around anyone except Adeline and Andre, but with it being their wedding weekend, I'm not about to ruin their happy vibe.

Now, here I am, about to walk down the aisle in this beautiful dress, carrying this

beautiful bouquet in this beautiful setting, and the truth is that I can't wait to curl up in my pajamas later and drown my sorrows while eating a huge piece of chocolate cake I'll get from the resort's bakery.

The music begins, and we wait for Mary to give us the go signal. Adeline's bridesmaids begin walking one at a time, and I wait my turn. I turn around and force myself to smile. "Here we go," I say to my sister. Dad stands beside her, looking handsome in his dress shirt, tie, and slacks.

Maybe if I fake this happiness long enough, I can fake myself into believing I am truly as happy as I'm coming across to everyone else.

Mary points at me, my cue to walk down the aisle. A small part of me hopes I'll look into the wedding crowd and see Kevin sitting with his parents. As if he suddenly changed his mind and flew down for the wedding... for *me*. But I know that won't happen. Only the sadist in me wants to hold on to the .0001 percent chance of that fantasy coming true.

I walk toward the altar covered in pink hibiscus flowers, with the breathtaking view of the sparkling Caribbean Sea behind it. I smile at Andre, who looks as happy as can be. I wonder if he'll cry when he sees Adeline walking down the aisle next.

Taking my place in the lineup of bridesmaids next to the altar, I scan the small crowd to see where everyone sits.

Okay. The sadist in me is looking to see if Kevin changed his mind.

Dan and Kathy sit behind Mom. No Kevin in sight.

The music changes to an orchestral rendition of "You Are the Reason" by Calum Scott, and everyone stands as Adeline begins walking down the aisle. She has her arm linked through Dad's, and they smile at all the guests as they approach the altar. I see Andre wipe his eyes as he looks at Adeline with pure adoration.

I'm incredibly happy for them, but I'm also hanging on by a thread. My heart hurts for what could've been with Kevin. Who knows what could've happened if he didn't decide to give up on us? Yes, the only people here who even know about us are Adeline and Andre. Yes, I'm doing a great job of masking my emotions. But listening to the words the wedding officiant is now saying as she begins the ceremony has me biting my tongue.

At least I'll have a good excuse if I cry. It's my only sister getting married, after all, and I'm incredibly happy for her.

Still, I try to block out the officiant's words. Instead, I think about my boutique. Maybe I can be productive and mentally get some work done, and at the same time avoid breaking down in tears. It's a win-win!

Somehow, I manage to make it through the ceremony only having to dab my eyes twice. I never actually cried, but my eyes did get watery.

Everyone cheers for the newlyweds as they walk back up the aisle. Then Andre's best man and I walk together, followed by the rest of the wedding party. Now, we have to take wedding photos before the reception starts.

I go through all the motions, following Mary's directions, smiling for photos, and trying my best not to ruin anything for my sister on her big day. Once we're done with the wedding party photo session, I need a break.

I need a drink.

Instead of following the rest of the bridesmaids toward the big bar near the beach, I head inside the resort to a smaller bar near the lobby. I could use a little alone time before the wedding reception kicks off. I have enough time while Adeline and Andre take photos of just the two of them.

The air-conditioning is a welcome relief as I walk inside the hotel's lobby. Although it's beautiful outside, it's also hot, and standing out in the sun for the wedding ceremony and pictures made me a little sweaty.

As I walk through the lobby toward the bar, I think the heat is affecting my vision, too. Kevin has been on my mind all day, and now I see a man who resembles him at the front desk.

Wait. Could it be? Or is it the little sadist in me playing tricks on me again?

The man turns his head. When he sees me, he stills. And I stop dead in my tracks.

No fucking way.

Kevin smiles, and all the blood drains from my face. It's him. It's really him. He's here in Mexico...

He walks toward me, taking long strides, not wasting any time.

I'm frozen in place. My .0001 percent chance of happening fantasy has come true, but what should I say to him? As much as I imagined this scenario playing out, I never considered what I would do if Kevin changed his mind and showed up.

"Monique," he says as he stops right in front of me. His blue eyes look into mine as if he can see right through me.

"What—I mean why are you here?" The most obvious question is the only thing that comes to mind.

He looks down at the ground for a moment before looking back up at me. He looks sad and nervous. "I-I just had to come."

"Why?"

His hand reaches for mine, and the second he touches me, warmth spreads throughout my body as tingles settle in my belly. It's like déjà vu of the first time we shook hands in Belize.

Kevin looks me in the eyes and continues. "I made a

mistake, Monique. I've never regretted anything as much as I regret ending things with you."

My heart pounds in my chest. Am I dreaming? Am I hallucinating right now?

"I haven't been able to get you off my mind," he says, taking my other hand in his as well. "Last night, I talked to my mom on the phone, and she told me about the festivities for Adeline's wedding. As soon as she mentioned you, I knew I had to get down here. I booked my flight as soon as I hung up with her. It took a while for me to get here, but I'm here now."

Speechless, I'm overwhelmed with emotions. He's saying everything I wished he'd say. He regrets what happened between us and had to come here for me.

"Pinch me," I say, wanting to make sure this isn't a dream.

"What?" Kevin asks, utterly confused.

"Pinch me. I want to make sure this is real, that you're really here saying all the words I hoped you would say to me someday."

He just looks at me for a moment before saying, "How about this?" Instead of pinching me, Kevin's hands move up to my face, and he crashes his lips to mine.

I kiss him with all I have. My hands hold him, not wanting him to disappear suddenly. His kiss deepens, our tongues volleying back and forth, and I know this is real. Kevin is really here—for *me*.

We hold each other tightly as we kiss with fervor. This is what six months of pent-up sexual energy and three months of regrets look like.

"I need you," he says, then goes right back to kissing me.

"My room. We'll have to be quick, though."

I take his hand and lead him to the elevator. As we wait for it to arrive, I realize he doesn't have any luggage. "Did you pack a suitcase?"

He cracks a smile. "Yes. The bellhop's holding it for me. Since I came here last minute, they didn't have any rooms available tonight. So I'm staying in my parents' room."

Confusion washes over me. "Wait. So your parents know you're here?"

He nods. "Yes. And I told them what happened between us."

I feel as if the rug's been ripped out from under me. "I'm sorry... *what*?"

"Please don't be upset," he pleads. "They were actually really happy for us."

"But... but they didn't say anything to me today. They knew you were on your way?"

"Yes. I asked them not to tell you. I wanted to surprise you when I got here."

My mind is blown. Dan and Kathy *know*? "Did they tell my parents?" I ask, although I doubt they did. I'm pretty sure my parents would have said something to me if they knew.

He shakes his head. "They kept it a secret."

The elevator arrives, and after the doors slide open, we enter the empty car, and I push the button for the ninth floor. As soon as the doors close, Kevin and I are all hands, lips, and tongues, all over each other again. I can't believe he's here, kissing me, and we're on our way to my room. We don't have much time before we have to be at Adeline's reception, but we'll have enough time for a quickie to tide us over until later.

When the elevator arrives on the ninth floor, we stumble into the hall, then quickly make our way to my room. Nerves and excitement make me fumble with the key, but I manage to unlock the door. We burst into the room and don't waste any time.

"Leave my dress on," I tell him as I work to remove my underwear.

"Bend over the bed," he says as he pulls down his shorts.

Following his instructions, I bend over the edge of the bed with my ass in the air for him. I hear him unwrap a condom, and after a few seconds, he lifts my dress, then drags a finger between my legs.

"You're nice and wet already," he says as he inserts a finger.

I arch my back, reveling in Kevin's touch. "That feels so good."

He pumps his finger in and out a few times before he replaces his finger with his cock. I gasp as he slides in deep. "Yes!"

"God, I missed you," Kevin says before he starts moving at a steady pace. "I missed your sweet pussy."

I moan at his words and at how good he feels. I wish we had more time right now so we could take this nice and slow. Based on the rate he's going, he's aware of our time limit as well.

"Harder," I say, needing just a little more in order to push me over the edge.

Kevin not only pumps harder, he also reaches around and presses his finger on my clit. Between him rubbing my bundle of nerves and slamming himself deep inside me, I'm already on the verge of coming apart.

"I'm going to come," he says, taking me by surprise.

"I am, too." One, two, three more rubs on my clit, and I scream in pleasure at the same time Kevin's orgasm rips through him.

"Fuck, Monique," he growls as he comes.

Once we both come back to reality, he pulls out of me, and we begin getting dressed. I go to the bathroom to make sure I still look presentable for my sister's wedding. As soon as I walk back into the bedroom, Kevin wraps me in a hug.

"I missed that. I missed you. You have no idea how depressed I was these past few months," he says as he kisses my neck.

"I missed you, too," I reply, holding him close. "I'm so glad you came here."

Kevin pulls back and looks me in the eyes. "I'm not letting you go this time, Monique. We're going to make this work... okay?"

I nod my head and wipe the tears starting to pool in my eyes. What an emotional day this has been. "Okay," I manage to say before Kevin kisses me on the lips.

When he pulls away, he looks at me and says, "I love you, Monique."

I suck in a breath as my heart pounds faster. We've

never said these words to each other, but I've thought them dozens of times. I know in my heart that I'm in love with Kevin, so I tell him, "I love you, too."

His face lights up, and he kisses me once again.

We make our way downstairs just as the wedding reception starts. It's being held outside under a covered area next to the beach. My parents sit with Dan and Kathy, and they look shocked to see Kevin and me walking up to their table, hand in hand, while Dan and Kathy have knowing smiles on their faces.

"What?" Mom asks, trying to comprehend what she's seeing right now.

"Mom and Dad," I say, "I have something to tell you."

EPILOGUE

Kevin

"Babe! Can you open the door, please?"

My hands are full as I carry another heavy box up the front porch stairs. Somehow the door shut behind me, and there's no way I can turn the doorknob to get back inside now. Luckily, it doesn't take long for Monique to open the door for me.

"Thanks," I say as I walk in the house and carry the box to the bedroom.

Our bedroom. Now that I've made the move to Paris, Monique and I can finally live together.

It's hard to believe it's been over a year since we played that game of truth or dare that led to our first kiss... which quickly heated up and led to our first time having sex together. Our relationship has come so far since our vacation in Belize. We no longer have to sneak around and hide our secret fling from our families. Now, our parents couldn't be happier for us. I wasn't sure how my parents would take the news when I told them I was moving all the way to Paris to be with Monique, but they were elated, to say the least. Likewise, Monique's parents also couldn't be happier for us.

Since we rekindled our relationship in Cancun six months ago, Monique has not only become my best friend, but we've fallen deeper in love with each other, too. Living apart from her was difficult, but we managed to make it work for the time being. During that six-month period, she flew to the States to visit me, and I also flew here to see her. And now... now we're finally going to be together all the time.

"Was that the last box?" Monique asks, following me into the bedroom.

"Yeah, it was," I say, setting the box down with the others I already carried in. I notice a framed picture of us hanging on the wall. It was taken in Mexico at Adeline's wedding reception, and the two of us look content in each other's arms.

"I love that picture of us," she says, noticing that I'm looking at the photo. "You had just fucked me in my hotel room about an hour prior to that."

I laugh at her blunt comment. "Yes. Yes, I did," I say, thinking back to that hot moment we shared right after I arrived at the hotel. We couldn't keep our hands off each other. It was the first of many other hot moments we shared in Mexico.

I can't wait to have a hot moment with Monique later tonight.

I pull her into my arms and kiss her forehead. "I love you."

"I love you, too," she says, filling my heart with joy. "Cancun was fun."

"Yeah, it was," I agree, thinking back to all the fun moments we shared. I was only there with her for three days, but they were some of the best days of my life.

Now that I'm in Paris with her, though, I'm sure we'll make more wonderful memories together.

"Becca and Jack want to have us over for dinner this weekend," Monique informs me, changing the subject.

"That'll be fun," I reply. "Are they getting settled in their new place?"

"Yeah, they are. Becca said now that they've been there a week, everything's finally getting put in its place, and it's feeling like home."

Monique's good friend, coworker, and former roommate just moved out with her fiancé a week ago. They've been looking for a place, especially since their wedding date is approaching. They finally found a nice apartment they could afford and moved out just in time for me to move in. While I wouldn't mind having Becca and Jack as roommates, I'm more fond of having an empty house where Monique and I can do whatever we want, whenever we want, wherever we want without worrying about anyone else seeing or hearing what we're doing.

Monique turns to face me and runs her hands through my hair. "I'm so glad you're finally here."

"I'm glad I'm finally here, too." I look into her beautiful hazel eyes, then press my lips to hers.

Finally. No more hiding. No more sneaking around. No more living on different continents. No more excuses for Monique and me not to be together. This is exactly where I'm supposed to be, here in Paris with Monique—the love of my life. We've come a long way since our time in Belize, and I feel fortunate to have Monique as my partner in life. One thing's for sure—I'll live in pure bliss with Monique by my side, wherever we are in the world.

The End

ALSO BY C.L. COLLIER

The Vagabond Series

Passion in Paris

Seasons of Love Series

Holly

Summer Love (A Summers in Seaside and Seasons of Love Crossover)

Autumn (coming soon in the Love and Coffee multi-author anthology)

April (coming in 2024!)

The Salvation Society

Harbor

Summers in Seaside Series

Summer Magic

Summer Love (A Summers in Seaside and Seasons of Love Crossover)

Hot Vegas Nights Series

Playing Vegas

What I Never Knew Series

What I Never Knew

What I Never Knew I Wanted

What I Never Knew I Needed

Discovering Us Series

Stacking the Deck

Finding Our Rhythm

Worthy of Love

Meant to Be

Visit C.L. Collier's web site

THE VAGABOND SERIES

A collection of standalone travel romances written by various authors you love!

Finding True North by E.A. Pierce

A Polar Pursuit by S.E. Rose

Passion in Paris by C.L. Collier

Nights in Nepal by Tarrah Anders

Join the series' Facebook readers' group

Follow the series' Facebook page

Visit The Vagabond Series web site

COMING SOON FROM C.L. COLLIER

Hopelessly Devoted: A Romance Anthology to Benefit Women's Cancer Research - coming September 7, 2023

Love and Coffee: A Limited Edition Contemporary Romance Anthology - coming September 19, 2023

Let's Get Naughty 2: A Limited Edition Romance Anthology - coming October 24, 2023

Stud Finder: A Limited Edition Romance Anthology - coming February 6, 2024

C.L. Collier's newsletter - Stay tuned for more!

ACKNOWLEDGMENTS

I want to thank Margot Swan and all of the other Vagabond Series authors for working so hard on this series together! You're all great to work with. I love the idea of The Vagabond, and the stories are fun reads. Margot, I'm glad you came up with the series concept!

I'd also like to thank all of the authors who have helped me along the way. I couldn't do it all without your support! I feel lucky to have gained so many good friends in the book world.

Finally, I have to give credit to all of the places I mentioned in this story. Most of them are real locations I had the pleasure of visiting in Belize back in 2021 when my boyfriend and I were lucky to visit the beautiful country with his parents. We stayed at the Maya Beach Hotel, in the same room Monique stays in the story––the Kingfish Suite. The views of the Caribbean Sea from that room were truly stunning.

The Bistro is still one of the best restaurants I've eaten at to this day. And, if you read my dedication at the beginning of this book, we did see Dee Snider and his wife dining there one morning. It was our last day in Belize before heading to the tiny Placencia airport, and he seemed like a regular guy, who also appeared to know the owners. We didn't bother him at all, though my boyfriend's dad did try to act like he was taking a picture of the beach in order to sneak a picture of Dee. I snuck a picture of him from where I was sitting, too, but his back was to me. It was still pretty cool to see the lead singer of Twisted Sister sitting just a few feet away.

I mentioned in the story how a woman was selling souvenirs on the beach––this was a common occurrence and how some people make a living there. We saw several women doing this and befriended a couple of them. Jesiah was one I bought a couple of items from, and Adella was the other. We got to know Adella pretty well during our stay, and I hope she and her children are doing well.

And the dogs. There were two sweet golden labs who hung around the hotel everyday, and we enjoyed petting these pups whenever we saw them. According to the owners, they lived across the street, but always came over to lounge on the beach. The Bistro's cooks would also feed them scraps, so these dogs ate well! They refused the dog treats we bought at the store for them, which we thought was funny. I guess they preferred gourmet dishes instead.

To say our vacation in Belize was incredible would be an understatement, and I can't wait to return again someday. I highly recommend visiting if you can. The people there are kind, generous, and proud of their country.

https://www.mayabeachhotel.com/

ABOUT THE AUTHOR

C.L. Collier is a USA Today Bestselling Author who lives in the beautiful Pacific Northwest. She was raised in the Seattle area, and although she lives closer to Portland, Oregon now, she frequently visits the hometown she loves. When she's not writing, you can find her reading, watching her favorite sports teams, spending time with her family, or going to concerts. She likes her music loud, wine and coffee sweet, and her books steamy.

Click here to visit CL Collier's web site!